AMOS

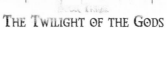
THE TWILIGHT OF THE GODS

www.amosdaragon.co.uk

First published in Canada by Les Intouchables MMIII

First published in Great Britain by Scribo MMX,
Scribo, a division of Book House, an imprint of
The Salariya Book Company
25 Marlborough Place, Brighton, BN1 1UB
www.salariya.com

Book Design by David Salariya

Printed and bound in Dubai

Cover Illustration by David Frankland

The text for this book is set in Cochin
The display types are set in CCNearMyth-Legends

AMOS DARAGON

BOOK THREE

THE TWILIGHT OF THE GODS

BRYAN PERRO

English Edition by
Glynne Yeardley

Scriba
A division of Book House

BRYAN PERRO

Bryan Perro was born in Shawinigan, Quebec, in 1968. He has trained as a drama teacher and actor, as well as obtaining a masters degree in Education. His best-selling series, *Amos Daragon*, has been translated into 19 languages (including English) and book one, *The Mask Wearer*, has sold over one million copies in Quebec alone. Perro has been awarded a variety of prizes for his fiction, including the 2006 Quebec Youth Prize for Fiction and Fantasy.

Amos Daragon
The Twilight of the Gods
Prologue

Since the dawn of time the Norsemen have told the tale of Ragnarök, a legend also called 'The Twilight of the Gods'. It tells of the events that will lead the world to the Apocalypse. The old storytellers and guardians of our ancestral traditions are most careful not to tell exactly what it is that will unite the forces of evil and lead to the final cataclysm. The world has been delicate and flawed since its creation and would be completely transformed by the rebirth of the Old Ones, the race of Fire Creatures.

For some time there had been reports that a mountain in the North had begun to roar. There were many reports of terrible goblin attacks on towns and villages. The Viking kings, Harald Blueteeth, Ourm Redsnake and Wasaly from Greenland ordered the setting up of a vast army to prevent the forces of Evil taking hold in the far off Northern lands.

All this was happening and the wise men scratched their heads for they knew that Ragnarök had begun and that only a miracle could prevent catastrophe.

In the great book of prophecies it is written that an elf would come to re-establish order. Accompanied by a great warrior, he would destroy the forces of darkness and bring peace to the lands of ice once more. But, as everyone knows, the elves have disappeared and great heroes are the stuff of fairy tales. The threat, on the other hand, is all too real. It seems that the stars have spoken and the world's destiny is sealed for in the distant Ramusberget mountains a dragon has been born. It stirs restlessly, stores up treasure and lays its eggs.

Soon there will be thousands more dragons.

CHAPTER ONE

THE BOAR'S HEAD

The first snowflakes were whirling around Great Bratel. The kingdom of the Knights of the Light was gradually preparing itself for winter. In the great capital city the inhabitants were chopping logs, draught-proofing their windows and checking their fireplaces ready for the cold weather. Soot blackened chimneysweeps ran through the streets. They were always busy at this time of year. They barely had time to finish one job before another customer called them. They went from house to house carrying their long ladders, picking up a few coins at each.

In the market square, women fought over the last few scraps of wool, their menfolk looked at the sky, making predictions about the coming season. They all agreed that it would be a hard winter. There would not be much snow but it would be very cold. All the signs were there.

The bees had swarmed lower than usual. The forest animals had thicker fur. Even the starlings, which were used to extreme cold, had flown off towards the South. The damp air felt unusually heavy and several children had already gone down with 'flu.

The Knights of the Light of Great Bratel wore wolfskins over their armour, but still they were cold. They shivered as they went on their traditional rounds of the city, hunched over their horses trying to absorb some of the animals' body heat.

Ever since the Gorgon attack that had virtually destroyed the town, there had been a new feeling of togetherness among the townspeople. Great Bratel was rising from its ashes like a phoenix. The people had been severely tested and had closed ranks. Their new lord, Bartholomew, ruled them honestly and justly. He had helped them rebuild most of the city. Once the crown jewel of the kingdom, the city was slowly returning to its former glory

The thick walls surrounding it had been rebuilt and reinforced. New look-out towers rose from the walls, stronger and higher than before. The guards who patrolled the walls looked out with satisfaction towards the setting sun. The last rays of sunlight bathed the great plain which surrounded the city, until the sun slipped below the mountain range in an explosion of vivid colour.

On the forest road, a few leagues from the city, the knights guarding the first checkpoint had a strange visitor. A weird-looking old man appeared. His head was shaven and he wore a thin white knitted woollen cap that, from a distance, looked like lace. He had a high forehead and slightly slanting eyes. His deep wrinkles seemed to make his tanned skin look even darker. The traveller had been baked by the sun and whipped by the wind for many a long year. His body looked like he'd spent many hours walking on difficult ground. His back was slightly bent and he wore his long black beard in a two-metre plait wrapped around his neck like a scarf. He wore an orange robe like a monk's habit. His clothes were spotless: without stains, tears or even a pulled thread. In spite of the snow on the road, the old man was barefoot. The snowflakes melted around his toes. He carried a simple bag slung over one shoulder and walked with a long staff tipped with an ivory spiral.

'Halt,' shouted one of the guards. 'Tell me your name, where you've come from and your reason for coming to Great Bratel.'

The old man smiled and shrugged his shoulders. His teeth were black and completely rotten. His breath stank strongly of fish, which forced the guard to step back hurriedly and clap his hand in front of his face. It was obvious that the old man was a foreigner who didn't speak their language.

'Pass old man!' said the other guard making signs as he spoke.

Turning to his companion he remarked: 'That old fellow doesn't look as if he'd give the town too much trouble! Look at him, he's limping on his left leg… poor old thing!'

The old man smiled again showing his rotten teeth. He had understood that he was welcome in the city and was pleased. He went through the checkpoint thanking the guards profusely in his own language and set off towards the city's main gate. In front of him was another checkpoint, manned by about twenty knights. A queue of merchants, travellers and citizens waited patiently to enter. The citizens of Great Bratel had always thought their city was impregnable but, since the Gorgon attack, they knew otherwise. The knights kept a tight watch over the comings and going in the city. They had all had a narrow escape and would never let anything like that happen again. It was soon the old man's turn to pass through the gate. A puny little knight stepped forward and asked him:

'Your name, nationality and business in Great Bratel?'

The traveller smiled sweetly and shrugged his shoulders once more. The guard swore:

'My God! You've got breath like a horse! Don't you understand our language?'

The old man just smiled foolishly, looking puzzled.He obviously didn't understand what the knight wanted.

'All right then,' said the knight. 'Leave your weapon here and you can pick it up again when you leave! Your weapon…yes, that thing…give me your weapon….Yes, that's right!'

The old man finally understood and willingly handed over his staff. He was given a small numbered metal disc, then he disappeared into the busy streets. He was tired from his long journey so he stopped at the corner of one of the quieter ones, took out a little wooden bowl from his bag and placed it in front of him as he sat down on the ground. He began to sing a traditional tune from his own country very loudly and quite off key. The passers-by quickly gave him a few coins – not to encourage him but to stop the dreadful racket. The old man smiled happily at his benefactors, displaying his teeth, thanking them with little nods of his head. Then, to the relief of the local shopkeepers, he wandered off.

He soon found himself at the door of an old inn called The Boar's Head. The owner had patched the place up as best he could since the Gorgon attack had demolished part of it. The building was only just habitable. It still had holes in its walls that had been roughly filled up and the thatched roof looked rather fragile. The traveller entered the inn, attracted by the smell of good soup, and sat down at a table. A dozen regulars fell silent and looked at him in disgust. The talk at the bar began again in a hostile tone. The place was dark and miserable and stank of damp. Dozens of flies buzzed around the tables and the customers' heads looking for a little warmth. The landlord came up to the old man and said:

'We don't serve strangers here so you can clear off!'

The old man gave his best smile and innocently held out his wooden bowl to the landlord. All the money he had been given in the street lay inside it.

'You pay good money for your soup you old devil! Very well you can have some broth! Do you want some nice soup then, you scum? Yes, nice soupee!' he sneered at his customer mockingly.

The old man laughed like a little child when he heard the landlord say the words 'soupee' and repeated it over and over, enjoying the sound it made. The landlord took the wooden bowl, took out the money and served the old man. He called to his customers:

'The old man's senile! Perhaps he's got some more money on him…. Make the most of it…times are hard and it's going to be a long winter!'

Three men got up. They were all carrying short sticks. The old man didn't seem to notice what was happening behind him as he sat hunched over his soup. He sipped it peacefully, smacking his lips after each spoonful. Three flies crawled around the table as the three men came close to the old man. Without lifting his head he killed the three flies with three precise blows from the back of his spoon. He moved so quickly they didn't have a chance to fly off. Three well-aimed little blows got them. Given how fast they could move, it seemed like magic. The three men stopped in their tracks, feeling less confident. The old man wiped the back of his spoon on his robe and finished his soup slowly, ignoring the three men behind him as they wondered whether to hit him or run away as fast as they could.

But the customers spurred them on, and one of them lifted his stick theatrically. At that precise moment the old man leapt to his feet, turning to face his attackers. With a slight smile he showed them his little finger, as if to say that he could overcome them with just one finger. This goaded them into attacking. The old man easily dodged the first blow and, with a tiny movement of his little finger, sent the stick crashing into the other thug's kneecap. A crunch of bone followed by a loud moan and a lot of swearing resounded through the inn. Using his little finger again he poked out the second thug's eye. Next he pushed the finger up the third one's nose and spun him round and round. The man fell unconscious to the floor.

In those three moves the old man had disposed of three strong and much younger men. He glanced at his attackers lying on the ground then raised his head towards the men standing at the bar. As if to invite them to fight he raised both hands and showed them…both his little fingers! The customers fled. In a few seconds only the landlord remained: frozen with fear behind the bar. His teeth chattered as if facing the most dreadful monster. Even the vile Gorgons had not had this effect on him.

The old man jumped lightly over the counter, pushed his forefinger into the landlord's forehead, closed his eyes and said, in a terrifying voice:

'Amos Daragon…'

In the old man's mind an image suddenly took shape: he could clearly see Amos and his parents sitting at a table in the inn. He read the landlord's mind. He could see a scene where the landlord had tried to cheat the Daragon family, the arrival of the Lord Bartholomew and the trick Amos had used to get out of trouble. He read all these details in the landlord's soul. Satisfied with the result of his action, he removed his finger and the landlord collapsed on the floor.

'It is difficult to penetrate the mind of a stupid man,' said the old man to himself in his own language.

He bent over the landlord's lifeless body, retrieved his money from his apron pocket, then cried 'Soupee! Ugh…' Then the strange old man discreetly left the Boar's Head Inn and headed quickly towards the North.

CHAPTER TWO

THE RED CAPS

T he town of Berrion was slowly coming to life early one cold morning. Here, too, they were making last-minute preparations for the coming winter months. At the castle where the Daragon family lived, Lord Junos had overseen the repair of broken chimneys and the hanging of extra tapestries to keep out the cold dampness of the stone walls.

In spite of the calm that reigned over his land Junos was worried. Ever since Lolya, the young queen of the Morgorians, had returned to her own country, Amos Daragon had been unwell. His health had been steadily worsening and in the last two months he had become dangerously ill. He had been seen by all the country's best doctors, but to no avail. His parents, Urban and Frilla, didn't know what to do next.

Amos did not sleep well. His dreams were full of ghosts and skeletons. He was haunted by images of a great city inhabited only by ghosts. He saw himself walking among them as if searching for something. He sensed that a terrible threat was hanging over the whole world, but he did not know what it was. He would wake up bathed in sweat, convinced that Lolya's knife had just been plunged into his body killing him. Amos could hardly eat and was often violently sick. He tried to doze by day but was always gripped by nightmares. He was haunted by terrible scenes of a suffering, desperate people. Sometimes he would see the face of a ship's captain, distorted with hate and howling curses. These dreams made his life unbearable. As the bitter cold of winter set in, he felt depressed and beaten. He coughed a lot, had difficulty breathing and hardly left his room. In spite of Frilla Daragon's tender care for her son, he grew weaker day by day.

Beorf Bromanson, on the other hand, was apparently in glowing health. The young manimal, the Daragons' adopted son, had put on weight. He was getting ready for winter in his own particular way. He belonged to the race of Beorites who could turn themselves into bears at will. He looked like any other boy of his age, apart from his two thick blond side-whiskers and eyebrows that met in the middle of his nose.

Beorf's parents had been executed by Yaune the Purifier, the former ruler of Great Bratel. Now he lived in the castle at Berrion under the protection of Lord Junos. Happily settled with his new family, he and Amos had become much more than just friends. He now had a real brother. Each night, Beorf stayed close by Amos keeping watch over him.

Since Amos found it so difficult to sleep, the two boys spent long hours talking together. Lolya's visit to the castle had caused strange things to happen and Beorf was convinced that his friend's illness was somehow linked to it.

One morning, as the first snowflakes began to whirl over Berrion, Beorf pulled back the curtains of Amos' room and said in a decisive voice:

'It's time we got out of here….Wrap up warm; we're going for a walk. I need some exercise and so do you – your parents and Junos all agree! It's a beautiful morning and the air will do you good. Come on, I'll help you…'

Amos lifted his head with difficulty and, protesting just a little, he slipped out of bed. Helped by Frilla and Beorf he tied his hair into a long plait and got dressed.

He fastened his black leather armour over some fox skins and slipped on his wolf's head earring. He looked drawn and had dark circles under his eyes. His face had a greenish hue to it and he was finding it hard to breathe.

As he walked towards the castle door he said quietly:

'I haven't told anyone this, Beorf, but I think I must be rejecting the Mask of Fire…'

'What do you mean?' asked Beorf. 'You had no problems when you put on the Mask of Air….Why should the Mask of Fire be any different?'

'I'm not sure. You know I've got to find another two – the Mask of Water and the Mask of Earth – plus fourteen more stones of power to set into them. And you know how they have to merge into my body to give me their magic – well I think I must be too young to absorb it all. The Mask of Air and the first stone didn't bother me much, but this Mask of Fire and its first stone are burning me up inside.'

'What are you saying?' asked Beorf, worried.

'Sometimes it feels as if my body's on fire,' replied Amos. 'It's agony. I get great blasts of heat that seem to soak up all the water in my body. My mouth is always so dry. I drink gallons of water but I'm still very thirsty.'

'Why don't you talk to your parents?'

'I don't want to worry them,' sighed Amos. 'All this mask-wearer business and the stuff about restoring the balance of good and evil, these nightmares and being so ill – it's just too much for them. My parents are simple people and they don't understand what's going on. What's happening to me is way beyond them …me too, if I'm honest. I feel as if everything's rushing towards me…and…well, I'm not really me anymore.'

The two boys walked on in silence, each deep in thought. They crossed the market square and headed towards the city gate. It was a crisp morning and Amos breathed in deeply, enjoying the fresh cold air in his lungs. Beorf was getting more and more worried about his friend. He glanced at him surreptitiously and was pleased to see some colour back in his cheeks.

Amos spotted his father coming towards them on horseback. He had a bushy beard and a dazzling smile. He waved vigorously to the boys, his eyes shining with pride at the sight of his two sons. As he trotted towards them there was a sudden whistling sound. Urban Daragon remained upright in his saddle for a moment before falling helpless from his horse. He hit the ground hard. Shocked, Amos froze for an instant, then ran to help his father. Immediately on the alert, Beorf tried to work out where the sound had come from. The bolt from a crossbow had struck Urban in the back of his neck, killing him instantly.

Beorf suddenly shouted, 'Look! There – on top of the wall! Look out Amos! He's reloading!'

Amos turned to see a hideous creature slotting a new bolt into his crossbow. The guards who usually patrolled this part of the wall were missing. They must have been ambushed or killed as they made their rounds.

The creature had a human body, but with long arms and short legs. Its skin was dirty brown and it had a large eagle-like nose, bulging eyes and drooping lips. Long thin fangs protruded from its lower jaw. It had large pointed ears and wore a red cap over its thin, straggly white hair. It wore coarse leather armour, metal boots and a wide belt from which hung a roughly hewn knife.

Loading its weapon, it took aim at Amos. He realised instantly that his father had been shot by mistake. The mask wearer had been the real target. Tragically, Urban had crossed the bolt's path just at the wrong moment.

The crossbow's second bolt shot towards him. Insane with grief, Amos let out a resounding yell and raised his hand towards the vile creature. A ball of flame leapt from Amos' body and burst towards his enemy, burning up the bolt in mid-flight. The red-capped creature was thrown into the air and was burnt to a crisp before hitting the ground. Beorf yelled:

'They're everywhere! They're invading the town!'

Turning himself into a bear, the young manimal ran towards the castle to raise the alarm. He was right: the streets had been overrun by the Red Caps. They seemed to have appeared from nowhere. They had opened the gates and were pouring through the streets of Berrion in a wave of evil. Armed with halberds, they had set about massacring the townspeople.

As he looked at his father lying dead at his feet, Amos was filled with an all-consuming rage. A dozen or so of the Red Caps circled round him. Instinctively he stretched out his arms and gritted his teeth. Tongues of flames spurted from the palms of his hands and, as he spun round, all his attackers died in agony.

In the market square, fifty or so Red Caps ran from stall to stall, looting goods as they went. Amos raised his right hand to the heavens and uttered a terrible cry of fury. In an instant a large pall of black smoke was all that remained of the creatures, the market tables, the fountain and three house fronts.

Panic reigned in Berrion as everyone fled as fast as they could. A long bugle call rang out and a hundred horsemen galloped from the castle, but they were of no use against the thousands of Red Caps now swarming into the town. As they came they robbed every house and shop of anything valuable: gold, silver, copper or bronze, and in particular, precious stones. They killed men, women and children before stealing from their bodies. They carefully selected rings, earrings, necklaces, birthstones and fine girdles from their victims.

Each member of this hideous army seemed to have a precise role. Red Caps with halberds were killing people, others pillaged the town, filling big cloth bags with their booty. Unarmed servants took the bags out of the town and brought them back empty for a refill. Sentries, armed with crossbows, protected the bag-carriers and killed anyone who dared approach them. They were organised and efficient and worked with utter cruelty. Each task was carried out quite inhumanely, as if it were simply a routine job.

Like a hurricane raging out of control, Amos roared through the town sweeping all before him. Red Caps rained down, crashing onto the rooftops. Some were thrown over the town walls others were impaled on the branches of nearby trees.

Suddenly, Amos was under attack, forced face down on the ground as three of the creatures raised their halberds to kill him. As he struggled to free himself the young mask-wearer turned into a human torch. His attackers quickly released him as they, too, burst into flames and ran off howling. Maddened by the sight of such awful destruction all around him, Amos roared with all his might:

'That's enough!'

Immediately all the wood in the town – floors, roofs, furniture, the handles of tools and weapons, carts, carriages, chariots, barns and trees – burst into flames. Without knowing how or why, Amos' cry had caused the entire town to be consumed by flames. His powers seemed to have been increased five-fold by his fury. The illness that had been eating him up for months now burst out of him, wreaking havoc. He had been taken over by the magical powers surging through him. Nothing could stop him; he was no longer in control.

Everyone, townspeople and Red Caps alike, fled towards the gates of Berrion. The furnace-like heat was unbearable. Amos careered through the town like a devil in Hell. He howled like a wild beast as he whirled around. Jets of flame poured from his mouth with every breath. His hair, now loose from its plait, flew around him.

He seemed to have gone mad! He looked around, relishing the sight of the burning town. The flames appeared to be made up of thousands of tiny men devouring Berrion. They sank their teeth into the wood, rejoicing in such a splendid feast. These tiny men were made almost entirely of molten volcanic lava. They had little breeches of glowing coals and hair of blue flames. One of the tiny creatures came up to Amos and knelt respectfully in front of him. Smoke poured from his mouth and ears as he raised his voice so he could be heard over the crackling flames:

'Choose us Master, for we are good people! Good people! Very good people! We have no god and we deserve a leader like you.'

Amos felt stunned and could not make sense of what he was seeing. Exhaustion crept over him. Struggling to understand, he stared at the little lava man, wild-eyed:

'What are you saying? What's happening here?'

'We are good people!' replied the little man. 'You were a god….The fire people know things. We know things that you have forgotten…'

'What have I forgotten?' asked Amos. His eyes were half closed and his head felt leaden.

'The Key of Braha!' replied the speaker, nervously. 'The fire people know things about the past as well as things of the future that have not yet been! You have fire and air within you! Come, be our god; come back to Braha and be our god! We are good people! Good people I tell you!'

Amos felt an overwhelming tiredness engulf him. His legs could no longer support him. His body keeled backwards as he fell heavily to the ground, unconscious.

CHAPTER THREE

RETURN TO THE FOREST OF TARKASIS

Amos strained to open his eyes. He found himself lying in a clearing carpeted with bluebells. He was wearing a loose garment of finely woven linen mixed with moss. Lifting his head he found a troupe of tiny blue fairies sitting on his chest watching him intently. They had long delicate wings and small pointed ears. They could easily be mistaken for dragonflies. Amos asked hesitantly, 'Where am I?'

One of the little blue fairies flew up to his face and hovered there, beating her wings very fast. She examined his eyes and said,

'Have you heard the bluebells ringing, young mortal?'

'I'm afraid I don't understand what you mean.' replied Amos.

'He doesn't understand what I'm talking about!' the

fairy laughed to her companions. 'Those who hear the ringing of the bluebells remember it – but not for very long!'

All the other fairies sitting on Amos' chest laughed, making a tiny tinkling sound. They flew off nimbly leaving behind faint trails of light.

'You should know that the flowers all around you are known as "the bells of death". Those who hear them ringing are hearing the tolling of their own funeral bell. They are magic flowers with great healing powers. The whole forest of Tarkasis draws its strength and powers from this clearing...'

'Ah, so am I in the land of Gwenfadrilla once more?' asked Amos feverishly.

'Yes,' replied the fairy. 'My sisters have gone to tell her that you have woken. Our queen will be expecting us. We must not keep her waiting. On your feet – quickly!'

Amos had difficulty standing up. His muscles ached and it took a huge effort to make his limbs work. The boy could see that the grass where he had been lying was completely flattened.

'I must have been here quite a while,' he murmured to himself.

He followed the little blue fairy for a short way through the trees before finding himself in the middle of the forest of Tarkasis. He recognised the place. It was where he had received his quest; it was here too that Gwenfadrilla had given him the Mask of Air. He recognised the circle of seven standing stones and the many strangely shaped wooden seats. During his first visit he had seen fairies both large and small, old bearded men, pretty young druid maidens as well as several strange, wrinkled dwarves. Today, however, the council chamber was empty.

The blue fairy pointed to a seat and Amos sat down. Suddenly, in a burst of light, Gwenfadrilla appeared before him. The Queen had pointed ears and wore a loose-fitting green gown. Her long fair hair had been shaved off leaving her completely bald. She smiled tenderly at the boy and came to sit beside him.

'Gwenfadrilla is happy to see you again, young mask wearer!'

Amos remembered that she always spoke of herself in the third person.

'What happened to your hair?' he asked.

'Gwenfadrilla has sacrificed it to protect her kingdom from the Red Caps. A fairy's hair carries great magic, and the ruler of this kingdom has had to spread it all around her forest for its protection. Do not concern yourself, my young friend, Gwenfadrilla's hair will never grow again but she likes the way she looks.'

'You are even more beautiful!' Amos complimented her kindly.

'You are very sweet,' said the Queen, smiling. 'Gwenfadrilla is very fond of you but she must bring you bad news.'

'I already know!' said Amos lowering his head and clenching his fists. 'My father is dead and I swear…'

'Calm yourself!' ordered the Queen in a commanding tone. 'Your emotions have already caused a great catastrophe in Berrion and Gwenfadrilla has no desire to see her forest ablaze. Allow her to explain…'

Amos nodded his head and listened carefully to the Queen's account.

'First, Gwenfadrilla must tell you about the Red Caps. These evil creatures are some of the wickedest and cruellest on Earth. They come from the ancient goblin races. Thousands of them live in ruined castles, choosing those with a history of vice, impurity and filth. They stain their caps red with the blood of the innocents they have slaughtered. They are disciplined and well organised and are deadly in combat. They have no fear of dying or of pain. Also…'

'But why did they attack Berrion?' interrupted Amos.

'As Gwenfadrilla was about to tell you,' she continued, 'the Red Caps live on what they can loot. They are building up treasure; a mountain of gold. Gwenfadrilla can see by your face that you are burning to ask her a question…. Well then, go ahead!'

'I don't know how to explain,' said the boy carefully,

'but I'm sure they are working for a dragon and that they are gathering treasure for it. Am I right?'

Gwenfadrilla seemed surprised but said,

'You are astonishing, my young friend! How do you know that?'

'I really don't know,' confessed Amos. 'For a time now...well, really ever since the day Lolya came to Berrion, I could tell she was possessed by an evil power until I tore a stone from her throat. This all sounds very confusing and it's hard to explain...I seem to have...premonitions. I know what I have to do and when I must do it, but I don't know how I know!'

'Listen to Gwenfadrilla, young mask wearer,' said the Queen very seriously. 'You are right. We were told by elves that a dragon has hatched in the North, in the land of ice. We thought the dragon race had been wiped from the face of the Earth but apparently it has returned. The Red Caps looted Berrion and a host of other cities because they are working for the dragon. The Old Ones – that's how the fire creatures were known – need to lie on a bed of gold, silver and precious stones in order to lay their eggs. The dragon has certainly bewitched the goblins into gathering the treasure. You must follow the Red Caps so that they lead you to the dragon. Then you must do as you see fit. Your mission is to re-establish balance in the world. Whether the creature lives or dies is for you to decide.'

'But what has happened to my mother? And Beorf...and Junos? I need to go back to Berrion!'

'The city no longer exists,' the fairy reminded him gently. 'It was you yourself who reduced it to ashes. Don't you remember? For some reason that Gwenfadrilla does not understand, it was your fury over your father's murder combined with the power of your two masks that let disaster loose on the town. Gwenfadrilla's fairies have searched the rubble but did not find Junos' body. However, she is certain that the Red Caps carried off your mother to sell into slavery. It's another way for them to get more gold for their master.'

'What about Beorf? Is he still alive?'

'Yes, he's still alive!' said the Queen reassuringly. 'You owe him a great debt. He risked his life to search for you among the flames. He carried you away from the town as everything was crashing around you....He came here to the edge of Tarkasis forest to ask for our help. Mastagan the druid had spoken of him and we recognised him as soon as he arrived. He was terribly burnt and we helped him to get well. He stayed at the forest edge and is waiting patiently for you to return. We carried you to the bluebell clearing to take care of you.'

'Beorf was not allowed to enter the forest?'

'Certainly not!' replied Gwenfadrilla. 'Even if he is a trustworthy young manimal we think it safer for us. In any case you have been here for ten days! Your friend would have been a prisoner here in the forest. You were difficult to heal; it's almost a miracle that you are still alive!'

'Ten days!' exclaimed Amos. 'That means that the Red Caps are ten days ahead of me. I must catch up with them as soon as possible! I've no time to lose if I want to see my mother again!'

'That is so,' agreed the Queen, 'but before you go Gwenfadrilla has a present for you and your companion, Beorf.'

As she spoke Gwenfadrilla clicked her fingers. A dozen little fairies flew towards her. They were carrying a small box made of red wood. The queen thanked them, took the box and opened it. Inside were four pointed, elf's ears made of crystal.

The queen turned to Amos offering the present saying: 'These may help you....These ears are powerful magic objects which will allow you to understand and to speak all languages. You will need them to be able to speak with the creatures that you meet so they will aid you greatly in your search! Keep one pair yourself and give the other to Beorf. They will also protect you from all magic chants.'

'They're wonderful!' exclaimed Amos.

'Gwenfadrilla must warn you of one thing: you must wear them over your own ears which will be transformed into real elf's ears.'

Amos slipped the magic ears over his own and in an instant his ears took on the narrow, pointed shape of the crystal ears.

'Can you hear what Gwenfadrilla is saying to you?' asked the Fairy Queen.

'Yes, very well!' replied Amos

'Did you realise that the Queen was speaking to you in the language of the fairies?' she continued.

'And I'm answering you in the same language!' cried the boy, proudly.

'Yes you speak our language with a charming accent! You can take the crystal ears on and off as you wish. However, always remember to hide them under your hair when you wear them or people will take you for a real elf.'

'I will remember,' the young mask wearer assured her. 'Thank you!'

'You must go now. Your true quest begins today,' said Gwenfadrilla as she left the council chamber.

Amos was guided by a bluebell fairy until he reached the long corridor of branches leading out of the forest of Tarkasis. He took off the robe of linen and moss and put on his fox skins and black leather armour. He had become acclimatised to the constant warmth of Gwenfadrilla's kingdom and was shocked when he felt the icy dampness at the edge of the forest. The countryside was buried in snow.

Amos called Beorf but got no reply. It had been mean of the fairies to abandon his friend out in the cold without food or shelter, he thought. Looking down at the ground, he saw footprints in the snow. He followed them until he came to a great hole dug under the roots of a tree. Bending down he peered into the opening and spotted Beorf curled up into a ball at the bottom of the hole. He was snoring peacefully, his body warmed by its thick layer of fur. Amos burst out laughing and said to himself:

'Silly old Beorf! He never told me that man-bears could hibernate!'

CHAPTER FOUR

THE ROAD NORTH

'Wake up Beorf!' cried Amos, shaking his friend vigorously. Beorf groaned a little, turned over and went straight back to his dreams. Amos climbed out of the hole and scratched his head. Just how do you wake a hibernating bear? Suddenly he had an idea and said in a loud voice:

'Hey! Not more pies and chicken? I'm sorry, but I just can't eat any more! If only Beorf were here…he'd just devour it! All these wild berries…juicy roast meat…mountains of nuts and so much honey – it's just too much!'

In the blink of an eye Beorf's head popped up from the opening of his den. His hair looked like a mop head and his eyes were still half-closed with sleep. He yawned: 'Pies? Chicken? Nuts and honey?'

'Well now, I've discovered the only way to wake a

Beorite from hibernation! It's all about your stomach, Beorf!'

'Meat?' he asked, still half asleep. 'I'm sure I heard someone say "meat"!'

'Come on. Up you come!' said Amos helping him to his feet. 'There's a little stream near here. We'll break the ice and the cold water will soon wake you up!'

'Oh yes, cold turkey would be lovely!' muttered Beorf as he stumbled along.

Beorf soon recovered his senses and the two boys wept together over the death of Urban. As they sat on the river bank Amos talked at length about his father, remembering all the good times they had spent together. He kept thinking of Urban's love and kindness. Beorf, an orphan himself, understood his friend's sadness completely and tried to comfort him as best he could.

After a while, Amos shook himself: 'Right, now we must set off after those evil Red Caps! They've taken my mother to sell into slavery and I'm not going to let that happen…'

'What happened in Berrion?' asked Beorf. 'Do you remember setting fire to the town?'

'Yes,' answered Amos lowering his head. 'Gwenfadrilla told me what happened. I don't know how it happened, Beorf. I was just so angry that my powers got super-charged. I destroyed everything without meaning to...'

'The mule! I've forgotten the mule!' shouted Beorf with great agitation. 'Follow me! Quickly!'

Beorf dashed back to the edge of the forest with Amos hard on his heels. After a few minutes the boys came upon an abandoned cottage. The young manimal opened the door and was immediately knocked onto his backside by a starving, furious mule obviously desperate to get outside. Beorf leapt up, ran to the back of the cottage and flung down a great heap of hay and oats for the poor creature. The mule began to munch greedily. Beorf wiped his forehead and said:

'I thought he might have died of hunger. I'd completely forgotten about the poor thing!'

'You'll have to explain. I don't understand anything!' sighed Amos.

'It's quite simple. When the fairies carried you into the forest, I went back to Berrion to grab what I could to help me survive. Junos once told us that he was born in a cottage near Tarkasis forest. I needed somewhere to put all the stuff I'd found, so I searched for Junos' old home and came across this deserted cottage. Perhaps it was his childhood home...but someone has been living here more recently...there's still some animal fodder. That's how I came to put the mule in here but as you know I fell asleep under the tree...'

'I see!" said Amos, laughing. 'The mule will be useful on our journey.'

'Come and see what I found!' called Beorf proudly.

In the cottage there were large tapestries which could be used as tents, some stout rope, some blackened oil lamps, several rusty swords, clothes, arrows and two bows in perfect condition, containers to carry water, embossed helmets, some fire-damaged furs, pieces of armour and coats of chainmail. Beorf had also managed to save the book called Al-Qatrum: The Territories of the Netherworld, which had once belonged to his dead father. This great book had been most useful during the episode at Great Bratel and could well prove valuable in the future.

The two friends prepared themselves for the journey North. Amos wrapped his feet and ankles in furs, cut up the tapestries to make a portable shelter, stuffed bits of fur into a metal helmet to keep his head warm and made a cape out of another brightly coloured tapestry depicting a coronation scene. He was finally equipped to face the terrible cold. Then choosing a sword without a sheath, he tucked it into his rope belt.

Beorf put a chainmail coat over his ordinary clothes. The manimal already had a winter covering of fur all over his body. From every angle he seemed to be wearing a perfectly fitting bearskin. He loaded up the mule and the two friends set off.

During the next two weeks of travelling the boys met with nothing but misery and desolation. They followed the Red Caps' trail through towns and villages that had been destroyed, burned and looted. The inhabitants had either been killed or, like Frilla, taken prisoner to be sold as slaves. The further north they travelled, the worse the Red Caps' attacks seemed to get. They became more and more cruel to their victims. Amos and Beorf found some of the sights unbearable. They began to have horrible nightmares and had an overwhelming feeling that they were being watched by an invisible, sinister, evil presence.

Every evening, Beorf stood guard while Amos searched for food. When Amos got back to the camp carrying some fish and a pheasant he found his friend curled up asleep under a tree. Beorf fell asleep more and more frequently. He was always tired and needed to rest. His hibernation instincts made him less hungry and more bad-tempered, especially when woken each morning. Amos did not like his friend's new behaviour, but realised he was fighting his bear instincts as best he could.

Amos was preparing the food while Beorf snored. He lit the fire by clicking his fingers and concentrating hard so that a little breeze kept the flames going steadily. The sun had almost disappeared behind the mountains. It felt as though it was going to be even colder tonight. Amos shivered as he watched the fish and game sizzling. As he looked towards the horizon, admiring the pale crescent moon, his attention was caught by a far off glow. He saw light shining from a castle, far off in the depths of the forest. Amos turned to Beorf and shook him hard.

'Wake up, Beorf, I can see a light over there! Someone must be alive! Perhaps they can tell us which way the Red Caps went! For goodness sake, wake up! We've had two horrible weeks….We can ask for shelter….Maybe even sleep in a decent bed…'

'Sleep in a bed!' cried Beorf, looking up. 'I'm on my way! Don't waste time – leave our stuff here. Let's take the mule and pray for a nice bed!'

After a good hour's brisk walking through the forest, Amos and Beorf reached their destination. They found themselves in front of strong walls surrounded by a deep ditch that could only be crossed by a narrow worn-out bridge. The moat and walls protected a large stone dwelling with a very high tower. Tired and grumpy after his late night march through the forest, Beorf lunged forward. Amos opened his mouth to warn him to take care but the words didn't have time to pass his lips. Too late! A plank cracked under the manimal's weight. He lost his balance, fell flat on his face and crashed through the drawbridge. He yelled out as he landed in the ditch amid the dreadful sound of splintering planks. Amos stepped gingerly onto the bridge, trying to see exactly where his friend had landed:

'Are you all right Beorf? Are you hurt?'

Amos was worried. He decided to use his magic powers to make a small ball of light in order to see where Beorf had landed. But before he could do that a metre-wide ball of blazing light appeared above his head. Amos could see Beorf quite clearly now, sitting at the bottom of the ditch. All around him in the snow were hundreds of gold coins sparkling like stars. Beorf squinted up at his friend and yelled:

'We're rich! There are thousands of gold coins here! No – hundreds of thousands! The whole ditch is full of gold…I can't believe my eyes!'

'Just touch one coin and you die!' thundered a deep voice.

Amos spun round in time to see a tall man wearing a wide brimmed hat and a long leather coat throwing a rope down to Beorf. In the bright, luminous light he could see the man's long red hair and big hands. He spoke with a strong accent:

'You there! Yes, you in the ditch! Grab this rope and climb up! And you, the young man on the other side of the bridge, walk along the right-hand side and you'll be safe to cross!'

The boys did as they were bid. The man spoke in a more reassuring tone:

'I was expecting you! I spotted your campfire as I was stargazing on top of my tower. I watched you through my telescope as you took the mule and headed this way. Come in…follow me. Dinner's ready. Ah yes. You can leave your animal on the other side of the ditch. He's quite safe from predators round here. They never come near my house. They're all afraid of me…'

Beorf and Amos looked at each other nervously. The man clicked his fingers, and extinguished the ball of light. The boys followed the strange man into the castle. Inside it was richly decorated and very luxurious. Huge portraits of ladies and gentlemen in courtly dress hung on the walls. The room was lit by dozens of chandeliers and heated by a fire blazing in an enormous fireplace. The furniture was old and made of exotic woods, and around the rooms were displays of gold statuettes, silver trinkets and many other costly articles. All the mirrors had precious stones set around them. The table was laid for three and covered with delicious food: rare fruits and roast meat. Beorf turned to Amos and whispered in his ear:

'This looks a bit better than your supper doesn't it? We should take him along with us as our cook!'

'Do take your places,' said the man taking off his hat and coat. 'Make yourselves comfortable, it's warm in here!'

After they had removed their winter clothes, Amos and Beorf sat down at the table.

'Eat! Make yourselves at home! Gorge yourselves! It's not every day I have visitors! You must be wondering about me….Let's start with this chicken while I tell you my story.'

Beorf didn't need to be told twice. His appetite had returned and the command to 'gorge himself' was sweet music to his ears! Amos, however, ate his food quietly while listening to the man's tale.

'This is my home,' he began. 'I belong to an ancient line of the De VerBoucs, a rich and noble family who own all the land around here. I am a duke…'

'And you're so rich that you just toss gold coins into your ditch!' cried Beorf cheekily gnawing on an enormous hunk of chicken.

'That treasure is cursed, my young friend. Whomsoever steals a single coin from that hoard of gold will find himself condemned to death.'

'And where does this curse come from?' asked Amos.

'It comes from a mad old man,' replied Duke De VerBouc. 'It goes back seven generations to when my ancestor made a pact with the devil….He swapped his soul for a sackful of gold. My ancestor was a miser of the worst kind. Owning land, villages, slaves and a massive fortune in livestock wasn't enough for him. He wanted gold; lots of solid gold coins.'

'But there's much more than one sack of coins in the ditch!' said Amos.

'That's because my ancestor tricked the devil,' continued the duke. He climbed to the top of the tower and made a great hole in an empty grain sack. He opened the sack and ordered the devil to fulfil his bond. Coins began to fall from the sky straight into the sack, but because of the hole it was impossible to fill. Hour after hour the devil continued pouring in coins. My ancestor laughed his head off at tricking the devil. A small mountain of gold began to rise at the foot of the tower. The devil had decided he was going to have my ancestor's soul whatever! Even if it should cost him millions of gold coins, he would keep on pouring until they reached the top of the tower and filled up the sack. As he watched all that gold falling from the sky, my ancestor cried out that he was richer than a god. But, at the very moment that the mountain of gold was about to reach the top of the tower and fill the sack, a violent waterspout appeared from nowhere and scattered the treasure. The waterspout carved out a deep ditch around the castle and thickly carpeted it with gold coins. The gods had punished my ancestor for his arrogance. He hurled himself down to the foot of the tower to retrieve his gold but broke his neck. The devil had lost my ancestor's soul as well as his personal fortune, so he placed a curse on his money. Since that day the De

VerBoucs have been forced to be custodians of the treasure. From generation to generation we are obliged to live here. We are allowed only one week in our lifetime to marry and bring about a new generation.'

'One week!' cried Amos in surprise.

'My poor son doesn't know that when he is eighteen he will have to take my place here. It will be a great shock for him, just as it was for me!'

'But what happens if someone steals a coin?' asked Beorf, wiping his greasy hands on his trousers.

'Once coins are taken away from the castle, the thief will die in a most horrible way. Ravaged by plague, black patches and huge pustules will slowly cover his body. Next comes delirium and vomiting and by then nothing can be done!"

Beorf gulped and took two coins from his pocket. Shyly he placed them on the table and said:

'I thought they might be useful on our journey, but now I come to think of it we don't really need money. Here, you can have them back!'

'Only two!' exclaimed the duke. 'If only someone were to steal the whole lot, the devil wouldn't need anyone to guard it and I'd be free. You will have to take a lot more than that young man if you want to help me! Why not fill up some sacks?'

'No thank you!' replied Beorf, laughing. 'I don't want pustules and black patches on my body either.'

'Well now, it's your turn. Tell me about yourselves and what brings you here.'

Amos explained how Berrion had been attacked by the Red Caps. He told of his father's death and their quest to find Frilla, his mother. He kept the secrets of Tarkasis forest and its fairies to himself. He also kept quiet about his own powers, the masks and his past adventures. Some things needed to remain a secret.

When he had finished, Amos saw that Beorf had fallen asleep in his chair. He felt his own eyelids begin to droop and he too fell into a deep sleep. The boys dreamt that they were sleeping in a comfortable bed between clean sheets.

Amos opened his eyes in the morning sunlight. He was sitting next to their smouldering campfire with the smoking remains of charred fish and a dried out pheasant. A little way off Beorf was snoring beneath a tree. There was no castle to be seen on the horizon and the morning air was icy. It was exactly as if they had fallen asleep in front of their campfire the night before and had never seen Duke De VerBouc's castle. As he stood up Amos saw an envelope at his feet. Inside he found a gold coin and a letter:

Dear Friends,
    It was a great pleasure to share my meal in such good company. You are welcome whenever you

wish to come again. Have no fear, this coin is not cursed. It will guide you to me if you should wish to see me once more. If I am no longer there, greet my son for me and tell him that I love him dearly and would have given my life to prevent our family's curse falling on him.

Your friend
Augure De VerBouc

CHAPTER FIVE

THE HOWLING HOUNDS

Amos and Beorf were completely lost. They had left the road several days ago to follow the Red Caps' tracks deep into an immense forest. It was a risk they had had to take – they had no choice: to find Frilla they had to follow those evil beings!

The forest was dark and gloomy. Giant grey pines obscured the sun all year round so the ground was icy and very slippery. The boys made slow progress – they had to take care not to fall on the treacherous ground. They also had to keep a look-out for signs which might help them track the Red Caps. These were not difficult to find as the goblins respected nothing, smashing everything in their path. Broken branches, gashed trees, small dead animals, smouldering campfires and all kinds of rubbish littered their trail.

Suddenly the two friends stumbled upon a body. It was one of the goblins. Amos examined the corpse and said to Beorf:

'He died in a fight. Look at these bites on his legs! He must have been attacked by some wild animal!'

Beorf scouted around for signs of danger and was startled to discover dozens of bodies.

'Look at this, Amos,' he called nervously. 'Your Red Cap didn't die alone…I think there are creatures in this forest that don't want to be disturbed!'

All around lay the savagely bitten bodies of goblins. It was a ghastly sight.

'I think we'd do well to keep a low profile!' said Amos nervously. 'It must have taken a lot of fierce creatures to have killed so many goblins!'

'I think you're right. Perhaps we shouldn't really be talking – you never know whether…'

Beorf became silent and began to peer into the treetops. His sharp ears had caught a strange sound. He scanned the trees and branches and then stared at something. He moved silently towards Amos and pointed to a strange figure.

'Look! There! Can you see it?' he murmured.

'Yes I can see something red up in the tree!' whispered Amos.

'I'm sure it's a Red Cap,' Beorf said through gritted teeth. 'He's sleeping astride a thick branch.'

'He probably hid up there when the creatures attacked,' Amos guessed. 'He hasn't dared come down again! I wonder how long he's been up there?'

'Suppose we get him to come down?' Beorf suggested. 'We could ask him a few questions! Listen to him snoring! I feel ready for a fight to stretch my claws.'

'I thought you hibernated in winter?' teased Amos. 'Won't it be a bit too much for you?'

'I'll sleep for a week to recover if I need to!' retorted Beorf crossly.

'Right then, let's go. It's time we found out what's been going on. Hold this rope, Beorf, and be ready to tie him up when he lands. I'm going to make him fall like a ripe fruit...'

Silently, stealthily, the boys moved across the icy ground to the tree where the goblin was sleeping. Amos concentrated hard and raised his hand towards the top of the grey pine. Gently, a little breeze began to blow on the creature's hat. It slipped from the Red Cap's head and began to fall. The goblin woke suddenly and instinctively tried to grab the hat as it fell. As the goblin lost his balance, Amos clicked his fingers and set fire to the bottom of his breeches. The goblin was so surprised by the sudden heat that he leapt off the branch, forgetting his precarious position. With a loud shriek, he landed flat on his face some fifteen metres below. He had smashed his nose and teeth on a huge tree root.

As he lay on the ground stunned, Beorf quickly stepped forward. In a few seconds he had disarmed the goblin and tied him tightly against the tree. Too shaken by his fall to defend himself, the goblin put up no resistance. Beorf held his claws to the prisoner's neck and said in a threatening voice:

'We're going to ask you a few questions and you're going to answer or I'm…I'm going to get very angry!'

'Aglack koi galok koi giss kuit!' cried the goblin in fright.

'I don't think he speaks our language!' reported Beorf, vexed.

'I have just the thing,' said Amos going over to the mule. 'I've got a present here from Gwenfadrilla which should do the trick.'

Then he took out the casket holding the four crystal elf's ears and showed them to Beorf. He explained their use and the two friends donned two pointed ears apiece. As soon as the Red Cap saw them he wailed:

'Elves. No hurting me! Me begging you, you no hurting me. Me nothing knowing!'

'Me asking you questions,' said Amos, who could now speak goblin language. 'You telling me what you knowing.'

'Me telling everything if you not hurting me!' offered the captive nervously.

'Me not hurting you! Me promising you!' agreed Amos.

'But me hurting you if you hiding me truth!' snarled Beorf showing his bear's fangs.

'First, you explaining me you dead brothers in forest and you in tree?' asked Amos.

'Dogs night attacking we! Everywhere dogs. Me protecting me, me climbing tree!' explained the Red Cap.

'You understanding?' Beorf asked Amos.

'Remove your ears!'

The two boys took off the crystal ears and heard the goblin ask:

'Gilka koi, puili kuit?'

'Just a minute!' Amos signalled to the goblin. 'Did you hear that Beorf? He's talking about black dogs.'

'Yes, I got that. What a strange language..."dogs night" means "black dogs"!'

'I think I understand what he's trying to tell us.'

Amos walked over to the mule and rummaged among their equipment and found the book Al-Qatrum: The Territories of the Netherworld. He quickly turned the pages and found a short description of the black dogs. It told how the animals commonly called the 'Howling Hounds' always lived in packs. They had black coats and were as tall as young bullocks and were easily recognised by their large, flame-yellow eyes. According to the book the hounds were guardians of treasure or protectors of sacred places.

'So you see, Beorf,' said Amos as he finished reading aloud, 'there must be some place in this forest that the dogs are jealously guarding. The Red Caps must have got too close to it without realising. These goblins paid with their lives for their mistake!'

'There were thousands of goblins when they attacked Berrion,' spat Beorf. 'A few dozen less is very welcome news. I hope the hounds eat them all before they leave the forest!'

'The only problem is,' continued Amos, 'they might attack us at any moment!'

'Kaquik mulf! Kaquik mulf!' screamed the Red Cap suddenly.

Amos and Beorf put on their elf ears again.

'You panicking, you explaining me...' asked Amos.

'Dogs night...dogs night all around we. We running! We running!' cried the goblin.

Beorf glanced round quickly. In the distance he could make out shadows moving and encircling them. Amos freed the Red Cap, saying 'You going! You free!'

'No with you!' cried the prisoner. 'Elf promise me: no hurting me. Me going you. Me following you – for protecting me!'

'We problems,' grumbled Beorf.

'We running!' shouted Amos in panic.

Amos seized the mule's reins and they began to run through the forest with the terrified goblin hot on their heels. The icy ground was slippery and the shadowy hounds were closing in. As he glanced over his shoulder Amos saw three enormous hounds with piercing eyes running ahead of the pack.

'We need to go faster. Leave the mule behind!' suggested Beorf.

'You're right,' panted Amos. 'according to the book, the hounds are guardians! The mule doesn't represent any danger to their treasure so the dogs would probably leave it alone. At least, I hope so.'

'But what about the goblin?' shouted the breathless manimal.

'If he follows us he has a chance to escape,' answered Amos. 'If not, then it's just tough!'

Grabbing a bed cover from their baggage, Amos let go of the reins and ran faster. Beorf had already turned himself into a bear and was running on all fours. The two friends arrived almost simultaneously at a huge frozen lake.

It looked like an enormous mirror lying flat on the ground. Behind them the hounds were getting dangerously close. Using his claws to grip the ice, the manimal was already bounding across the lake. Amos held two corners of the bed cover in each hand and using his special powers, he filled the improvised sail with wind. He took off so suddenly that he almost fell and only just managed to right himself in time. With both feet firmly on the ice, Amos was now gliding across the lake at a fine pace. Using his magic powers again, he warmed the soles of his boots to reduce their friction on the ice. In seconds his speed doubled and he had caught up with Beorf.

'Look over there!' cried Amos. 'There's a house on the far side of the lake! Let's shelter there.'

'The hounds...I can smell them! They...they're catching up with me!' replied the bear, panting.

'Grab hold of me Beorf!' shouted Amos, slowing a little. 'Hang on to my belt!'

The manimal seized Amos' belt in his teeth. Seeing the pack was not far behind them, Amos concentrated harder. Now powerful gusts of wind filled the sail carrying them both along with ease.

Beorf suddenly felt something seize hold of his back leg. He turned his head to find that the goblin had joined them. Had anyone witnessed the scene, they would have been astonished: a boy was gliding swiftly across the ice behind a sail that looked like a bed cover which was filled with wind, although the air was quite still. The boy was towing a bear on all fours and onto the bear clung a clearly desperate goblin. The unlikely trio continued to gain speed.

Just as had happened in Berrion, Amos had lost control of his magic. His fear of the hounds had let his emotions take over again. The gusts of wind had become a violent gale. The soles of his shoes were now so hot that Amos left two lines of boiling water in his wake. Clouds of steam billowed up from his feet. Once more, the power of the elements threatened to ruin everything. Aware of the danger they were in Beorf decided the trip had lasted long enough. He deliberately stumbled into Amos who fell flat on the ice. His concentration was broken by the fall and the wind dropped immediately.

They still had enough speed to carry them to the edge of the lake where they all landed head first in the snow. They were now only a few steps from the house that Amos had spotted earlier. In a few moments they would be safe from the hounds.

The building turned out to be a small temple. Once inside, Beorf barricaded the door and turned himself back into his human form. The goblin, who witnessed this, couldn't get over it. He had never seen a Beorite before and the change left him stunned. He sat on the floor, open mouthed, eyes like saucers, watching the fat boy with the pointed ears. Finally he dared to ask:

'You bear or you boy?'

'You keeping mouth shut!' replied Beorf, angrily. 'You keeping quiet or me gobbling you up!'

The Howling Hounds were all around the little temple now. Amos watched their movements through the window. The big, black dogs seemed very agitated. He called Beorf over and said:

'Look how nervous they are...I think we must be in the very place they are supposed to protect.'

'You telling me treasure for we here?' began Beorf. 'Oh, sorry with these elf ears I keep forgetting which language I'm speaking! What I meant to say was...'

'Yes, I understood!' replied Amos. 'I'm still wearing my crystal ears too. You're right. There must be treasure here. The hounds won't let us take it without a struggle though.'

'You speak language elf?' asked the fascinated goblin. 'We treasure here? Me understanding...'

'Me throwing you outside to dogs! You liking? Night dogs needing dinner!' growled Beorf.

Suddenly, a candle lit itself by the altar of the little temple. Amos muttered to his friend:

'I didn't do that. Get ready, there might be some action!'

Just then, in the opening to a room behind the altar, a druid appeared. He stood next to the candle and was carrying a gold chalice. It was a horrible sight: the man had no face, just a smooth white skull. This being, half man, half skeleton, dressed in ceremonial robes, began chanting in a low, calm voice:

'By Manannan Mac Lir, rightful son of Lir, husband of Fand, let us bring honour or let us die!'

'What's going on?' Beorf sounded anxious.

'I've no idea!' said Amos with a shrug.

'By Manannan Mac Lir rightful son of Lir, husband of Fand, let us bring honour or let us die!' repeated the druid.

'That's it! I think I know what he wants!' exclaimed Amos looking around.

'Tell me!' hissed Beorf.

'By Manannan Mac Lir rightful son of Lir, husband of Fand, let us bring honour or let us die!'

'You'll see,' answered Amos.

The boy stepped up to the altar. Just beside the hideous druid, a great book rested on a lectern. Opening it, Amos glanced rapidly through it. Thanks to his magic elf ears he could easily read the print.

'By Manannan Mac Lir rightful son of Lir, husband of Fand, let us bring honour or let us die!' intoned the druid yet again.

'Let us die with our heads held high in combat! Let us die as we have lived...without fear or humility!' Amos read from the book.

'Let the water carry us!' the skull chanted back.

'Let the wind lead us!' responded Amos with his eyes fixed on the book so that he could follow this very strange ceremony.

'Let the blood flow through my veins...'

'And let my enemy's blood flow likewise...'

The two voices kept alternating. 'Manannan Mac Lir', the druid repeated frequently, raising his skull with its empty eye sockets to the heavens.

'Great god of gods,' answered Amos, his voice trembling with emotion.

The ceremony continued in this way for nearly an hour.

As he blessed the disciples of Manannan Mac Lir, the druid turned to face Amos. But the figure no longer had a skull with empty sockets where there should have been eyes. Instead there was a luminous face with an expression of great serenity. The druid had a long beard made of seaweed and sea anemones of many colours. He said:

'I was condemned to return here each day until a kind soul should help me recite the service which I once neglected through greed and envy. Many have entered this temple in search of my fortune and have died at the fangs of the Howling Hounds. Take the gold casket which is under the altar. It contains my riches which I give to you so that you can continue your journey to the North. I have waited two hundred years for someone to free me. I have paid my debt to my god Manannan Mac Lir. I am going to him now and I shall seek his favour for you.'

When he had spoken these last words the druid vanished. Amos and Beorf looked underneath the altar and saw the casket. It was full of blue sapphires. Hundreds of them. Beorf grinned.

'I think we're rich, Amos!'

'I think so, too! We'll have no more money problems for quite some time!'

As Amos turned to Beorf he saw him fall heavily to the floor. The goblin had hit him over the head with his stick. Excited by the sapphires, the Red Cap's eyes were popping out of his head and he was drooling like a mad dog. Before the young mask wearer could react he, too, was hit over the head. Just before he passed out, he heard the goblin cry:

'Me riches! Me riches...me...'

CHAPTER SIX

THE TEACHER

Amos opened his eyes. He had a terrible headache, his lower lip was split and he had a huge lump on his forehead. Beorf, too, was gradually coming round. The mask wearer got to his feet, groaning:

'We've certainly been had!'

'Ouch!' exclaimed Beorf as he sat up. 'If I find that damned goblin, I'll knock his head off!'

'I suppose we'd better start tracking him to get our casket back,' suggested Amos, still dazed. 'We must catch him…'

'Yes, you're right.' agreed the manimal. 'Let's get going straight away!'

The boys left the temple quickly and, to their horror, found themselves confronted by the whole pack of Howling Hounds. They ought to have been chasing after the goblin! Amos and Beorf froze and began to back away. Facing them were a hundred big black dogs, but they were behaving oddly...they seemed curiously calm and among them was the mule, apparently unharmed and unconcerned. Slowly, the largest hound came up to Amos, head down with its tail between its legs and rubbed its muzzle against his hand. The dog was asking to be stroked! Beorf burst out laughing with relief.

The whole pack now came towards the boys wagging their tails. Just as Amos was bending forward to stroke each of his new friends in turn, a powerful beam of white light split the sky. The animals disappeared instantly and the young mask wearer found himself with a chain in his hands. Its links were made of walnut. One hundred dogs' teeth, exquisitely decorated with silver, hung from it. Amos looked at Beorf in astonishment.

'It looks as if we now have an army of one hundred hounds at our service. I've only to throw down one of these teeth and it will turn into a huge black dog! At least that's what it said in Al-Qatrum: The Territories of the Netherworld.'

'Well,' said Beorf, taking hold of the mule's reins, 'you're the first person I've ever known to wear an army round his neck! Let's hurry and catch up with that damned goblin!'

Once more Amos and Beorf set off in search of the thieving Red Cap who had made no effort to hide his tracks. They walked through the forest for hours, discussing Amos' difficulty in keeping control over his magic powers. The mask wearer couldn't understand what was happening to him. Never before had his magic been so powerful and so destructive. His emotions seemed to magnify the effects of even the simplest spell with disastrous results. Was it because of his long illness? How could he set things right? He needed to find some answers!

It was almost night when they saw a telltale light in the distance. As they got closer they spotted the thief sitting in a tiny clearing. The casket was resting in his lap as he warmed his hands at a campfire. Amos noticed straight away the goblin's behaviour was strangely exaggerated. The creature looked around furtively this way and that. It was obvious that he was playing some sort of trick and that he wasn't as cold as he made out. He must be expecting them. In the last dying rays of sunlight, Amos could see that the snow in the clearing had been swept. Tracks, possibly hundreds of footprints, had been obliterated. The Red Cap was just the bait in a trap. The scene was set for an ambush!

Unaware of the danger, Beorf turned himself into a bear and ran snarling at the goblin. Amos tried to stop him, but it was too late. The manimal ran straight into the trap. He had only taken a few steps into the clearing when dozens of Red Caps jumped down from the trees and pounced on him. In a few seconds he was captured, his paws bound and several halberds were at his throat. The Red Caps celebrated their catch with war cries and yelps of joy. The sapphire thief soon quietened them down.

'Showing you elf Amos to we or we killing he!'

Warlike yells rose from the troop of goblins. Hidden behind a tree, Amos fingered the chain at his neck nervously. An army of Howling Hounds could easily see off the Red Caps, but not before they had killed Beorf. What should he do? Should he use his magic powers once more and risk destroying everything? Give himself up and face death? Stay in hiding and see what happened? He had to save Beorf – but how?

'Showing you!' yelled the furious Red Cap pointing the blade of his halberd at the manimal's throat. 'If you playing tricks on we, me killing he! Showing you to we… now!'

Amos scratched his head. Usually, he knew exactly what to do even in the most difficult situations, but now he was terrified. Suddenly his body began to burn. The snow had melted all round him. On the ground just in front of him little flames danced, whispering:

'Choose us, Master, we are good people! Good people! Very good people! We have no god and we deserve a leader like you.'

The mask wearer was about to lose control of his

magic yet again! Just as he had in Berrion, he would be turned into a human torch! Soon, all of this part of the forest would burst into flames and a giant tornado would destroy his enemies. Revenge had begun to take the place of fear. Amos thought about his father's death and the kidnapping of his mother. And still the little lava men flames danced before his eyes murmuring:

'Choose us, Master, we are good people! Very good people!'

'Show you to we,' howled the goblin raising his halberd once more. 'Me cutting off he head! Me cutting off he head!'

'Good people! Very good people! Good people!' sang the flames like a litany.

'He die!' cried the furious Red Cap.

'He die!' chorused his horrible companions.

A piercing cry reverberated through the forest. For a few seconds, the terrified Red Caps froze. Amos recovered his senses immediately and looked up to see where that warlike roar had come from. Out of the forest, in a blaze of white light, sprang the strangest apparition. An old man alighted in the clearing. Clad in a loose orange robe, a white woollen hat and carrying a travel bag slung over his shoulder, he stood on a unicorn's back. He was skilfully twirling a long lance with a spiral tip. His plaited beard trailed two metres behind him. A ball of iron swung from the end of it.

Galloping at speed, the unicorn charged the group of goblins. It speared two goblins with its horn as it passed them, then flicked them off with a shake of its head. The old man, still on the unicorn's back, was spinning his plaited beard like a lasso. The iron ball on the end of it sent a dozen Red Caps flying, breaking arms, shoulders and ribs in the process.

In a move as elegant as it was hazardous, the old man did a double somersault off the unicorn and landed on his feet in the middle of the clearing. With three thrusts of his spear, he killed five Red Caps. Maddened by this, the goblins fought harder than ever to defend themselves. Wielding his weapon with incredible skill, the warrior avoided every blow aimed at him while each one of his struck its target. He seemed to know his opponents' weak spots and attacked their necks, stomachs or legs accordingly.

The sound of breaking bones, cries of pain and the terrible racket of moans and groans echoed in Amos' ears. Any goblins attempting to make a run for it were tossed into the air by the unicorn. The magnificent white beast galloped around the clearing to prevent any escaping. In three minutes it was all over.

The sapphire thief was the last goblin left standing. He backed away from the old man stammering incomprehensible excuses. Smiling, the old man looked into his eyes, and then let out such a piercing shriek that the Red Cap crumpled to the ground, stone dead. The intensity of the sound had pierced the goblin's heart.

The old man rearranged his orange robe back into place. Despite the battle, his clothes were without a single stain or tear. He went over to stroke the unicorn and murmured a few words in its ear. The animal nuzzled him lovingly then trotted off into the forest. Slowly, Amos approached the clearing. The goblins' bodies lay lifeless on the ground. There must have been at least a hundred.

The old man freed Beorf and, making a sign for Amos to come over, he said:

'Usually, clever people are not brave and brave people are not very clever! Well then, you are more brave than clever, Mr Bromanson. Your position here proves that….As for you, Mr Daragon, you were clever enough to see the ambush but not brave enough to rescue your friend. That is not good. On the other hand you both have very fine ears. That's a good sign because, where I come from, they say that a man who does not hear is out of control!'

'Who are you and what do you want?' demanded Beorf brusquely.

'He who is ashamed to ask questions is ashamed to learn!' said the old man, winding his beard round his neck like a scarf. 'That's good Mr Bromanson. That's very good indeed!'

'Yes,' said Amos thoughtfully, 'and those aren't the only questions that need answers, are they?'

'Marvellous!' cried the old man like a proud father. You are just as I imagined, Mr Daragon. Quick-witted! Alert! We're going to get on well, the three of us. We shall have fun together....Oh yes! We shall get on famously!'

'The three of us?' chorused the boys in surprise.

'Yes, that is correct' affirmed the old warrior. 'From now on I shall be your master...or should I say your guide! Now then! Who wants tea?'

CHAPTER SEVEN

FIRST LESSONS

The old man took a small kettle from his bag, poured in some water and put it on the campfire to boil. Then the boys helped him to remove the goblins' bodies from the clearing. It was dark now and the three of them were soon sitting round the fire drinking a fragrant tea. The old man tore a hunk of bread into three pieces and said:

'I must tell you a story so that you can understand why I am here with you. One day, as my teacher came in from a long walk, I asked him what was meant by knowledge. He held out a long staff and told me that knowledge was exactly like that staff. He had carved and polished it with his own hands. Now he used it every day to help him on his way. It's quite simple, I shall be like that staff to you because I shall support and help you on your journey.'

'Yes,' said Amos, 'but…why us? Why here? Where are you from? And who are you really? How is it…?'

'So many questions!' interrupted the old man. 'Let's begin at the beginning. My name is Sartigan and I grew up in the far off lands of Chû, in the distant eastern regions of the continent. As a young boy my parents gave me into the care of the temple of the god Liu. I lived my boyhood there in peace. The life was hard but I learnt a lot. I became a great fighter, respected and loved by all. I am, as we say in my land, a fire warrior.'

'What's a fire warrior?' asked Beorf, eyeing Sartigan's untouched piece of bread.

'A fire warrior is a dragon-hunter,' replied the old man.

'But dragons haven't been seen for thousands of years!' exclaimed Amos. 'You're certainly not a thousand years old!'

'Oh but I am! And I nearly died because of one of those terrible creatures. I was fighting with my troops in the north of the continent and during the battle I fell into frozen water. While the god Liu protected my soul, my body was imprisoned in the ice for hundreds of years. When I opened my eyes once again I was back in my own land on a lonely beach. That was almost thirteen years ago. On the exact day you were born, Amos.

'I came back to life to be your teacher and your guide. Liu gave me this mission. I set off and for twelve years I have been walking to meet you, the first of the new generation of mask wearers. Now I am at your side. It has been…a long road!'

'Were you a mask wearer, too, in those days?' asked Amos, much moved.

'Ah no!' laughed Sartigan. 'I was not so fortunate! I did once see a mask wearer at work though. Our army had asked him for help to fight a dragon. The beast was hiding in a cavern under a mountain. Do you know what the mask wearer did? He closed his eyes and concentrated and a great earthquake turned the mountain into a volcano. Later, once the lava had cooled down, we found the dragon's bones in it. His name was Arkillon and he was one of the greatest mask wearers the world has known. Like you, Arkillon was an elf.'

'That's strange…that name reminds me of something,' mused Amos.

'Perhaps you've heard it in old songs!' said Sartigan. 'He was a reformed thief. Legend has it that he had been placed under a terrible curse and lived as a prisoner in the Underworld.'

'Master Sartigan, sir, can I have your piece of bread?' asked Beorf at last, his mouth watering. 'As you're not eating it I wondered if…well…maybe if you gave it to me I could tell you a secret!'

'Very well,' answered the teacher handing him his portion. 'What is this secret that I must buy so dearly?'

'Well, you see, Amos and me – we're not elves!' he declared biting into the bread. 'You explain, Amos. It's rude to talk with your mouth full and as I'm eating…'

Amos took off his crystal ears. He was surprised to find that Sartigan wasn't speaking the same language as he was. The teacher was astonished to discover that he could no longer understand a single word that his new pupil said. Only Beorf understood them both, but he was too busy scoffing the last bit of bread to join in. Sartigan examined Amos' crystal ears and made a gesture asking permission to try them. To his great astonishment his own ears became pointed.

'Now you will be able to speak my language,' said Amos with a smile.

'If only I'd had these in my time…,' murmured the teacher, meditatively.

'They were a gift from the fairies of Tarkasis…,' added the boy.

'Yes…yes…I met those fairies. I came across them near Berrion or rather, I should say near what's left of Berrion! The little fairies couldn't understand why a dragon-hunter would wear such a bright colour! That made me laugh!'

'Why do you?' asked Beorf eyeing the teacher's bag furtively and wondering if there was any bread left.

'Gracious me!' cried Sartigan indignantly. He looked dismayed. 'Don't you know that dragons can't see the colour orange? You probably don't realise that my lance tip is made from a unicorn's horn, either?'

'No...,' said Amos with a shrug.

'It is the only weapon that can pierce through a dragon's thick scales! Swords and arrows cannot wound an Ancient One, but the ivory from a unicorn's horn can pass through anything.'

'How do you get hold of the horns?' asked Beorf, rummaging in his own bag for something to nibble.

'Don't you know anything at all?' exclaimed Sartigan in astonishment. 'I have come into your lives just in time! Well then, let's talk about unicorns! These magnificent creatures live in great forests all over the world. They are generally invisible to mortal eyes but sometimes they allow themselves to be seen by good, kind people and may even allow themselves to be ridden. Unicorns are amazingly strong and fast. All of their power is concentrated in their horn and at the point of death they may offer it to a mortal. That's how I was given this weapon...I've already been able to count one unicorn as my friend.

The teacher remained deep in his own thoughts for a while before continuing:

'In giving me this magnificent weapon the unicorn made me a friend of its whole race and that is why unicorns always come to greet me whenever they see me. Unicorns are my allies on whom I can always rely.

Do remember though, that a horn given freely by a unicorn retains all its power but a stolen horn is worthless.'

'People do hunt unicorns don't they?' asked Amos.

'Yes there are lots of hunters and poachers. They kill these superb creatures to steal their horn. It's no use wise men and magicians telling them that it's worthless, they don't believe it. All they want is the horn's power!'

'But if unicorns are invisible…how do they do it…how do the hunters catch them?' mumbled Beorf chewing a bit of leather to stave off his hunger.

'A good question Master Bromanson!' said the teacher admiringly. 'Unicorns have several weak points. First of all they are fascinated by their own reflection. Once attracted to a mirror they lose their powers, especially their invisibility. The hunters know this and place mirrors around the forest to act as traps. Secondly, unicorns have a weakness for the charms of innocent, young girls and love to be stroked by them. So hunters take their sisters along to coax unicorns out of their hiding places. By lying down to be caressed the unicorns become vulnerable and can easily be killed. The unicorn's last weakness is in battle. They know they can pierce armour easily so they always charge head first. An old hunter's trick is to stand in front of a tree and to step aside at the last moment. The horn goes into the trunk and the animal is caught fast in the tree!'

'But how do you explan...,' asked Amos.

'That's enough!' Sartigan interrupted him. 'We've talked long enough.'

'And not eaten enough.' grumbled Beorf

'Let's get some sleep,' suggested the old man. 'These goblins I got rid of are just a tiny, tiny part of an army that's travelling around these parts. We still have a long way to go if we're to find your mother, Master Daragon!'

'But how do you know that?' Amos began to say.

Sartigan cut him off once more, 'I know lots of things but I'm tired now!'

'We should have a lookout rota,' suggested Beorf.

'Don't worry about that...,' answered Sartigan. 'I have a friend who will keep watch! Here, Amos...take your crystal ears back. Be sure to keep them hidden when we leave the forest. I have heard that elves don't have a very good reputation among the peoples of the North. Good night! Oh yes...I was forgetting! Until I give further orders you are absolutely forbidden to use your mask wearer powers, Master Daragon! Remember...that's an order!'

Amos turned his head and saw the shadow of a unicorn eating some branches.

'One final thing before we sleep!' said the old man hastily. 'I know you Beorites, Master Bromanson. The more you eat, the more you sleep! Your race, young

man, can choose whether to hibernate or not. As I want
you awake and alert for our journey, from now on you're
on a diet, Master Bromanson!'

'What!' howled Beorf, aghast. 'Do you want me to
die? Is that it? I can't diet....It's...it's against my
nature...I...'

'Be quiet and get some sleep!' the old man ordered.

'I hate that man,' grumbled Beorf.

'I beg your pardon?' said Sartigan, sitting up again.

'I, er, hate...this place!' replied Beorf heading for
the mule to fetch some blankets. 'Its this place...I
hate it!'

'That's all right then, I thought I heard something
else...'

Amos made up the fire and as Beorf settled down, he
too lay down for the night. Sartigan slept on the frozen
ground, barefoot and lightly clad. The two boys fell
asleep under a magnificent starry sky to the sound of the
wind in the trees and the old man's resounding snores.

Amos suddenly saw his father's face appear before
him. The young mask wearer was in his bed in the
cottage where his parents once lived in the kingdom of
Omain. This was where he was born and grew
up. Urban had just woken him and Amos hugged
him lovingly.

'Listen to what I tell you, my son,' began Urban. 'It is a puzzle that you must solve for yourself. When I was young I had a fine horse. Its coat was flawless, its legs long and strong and it was without doubt one of the most intelligent beasts of its kind. Before my father gave it to me, he wanted to break it in properly. He tied it to a post on a very long rope. The young horse began to rear up and thrash around. Deprived of his freedom, he fought against his new master with all his strength. He reared up in the air, stamped his hooves, whinnied angrily and tried to bite anyone who came near....But the post was firmly fixed and the rope was so strongly made that he could not escape. He was beside himself with fury, but could do nothing. He was still tied to the post. For several days the horse wore himself out like this till one morning he calmed down completely. My father released him and gave him to me. For many years that horse was my best friend. We went down to the village or the river together and we would gallop wildly over the fields and through the forests. He helped my family and was always free to come and go at will. Do you understand what I am trying to say to you?'

'I think my powers as a mask wearer are like the horse in your story,' replied Amos. 'They take fright, fly in all directions in a rage because the magic feels imprisoned in my body. Is that why I lose control!'

'Well done, my son!' exclaimed Urban, stroking

Amos' head. 'It is your concentration that is the "rope" to hold your powers in check, and being in control of your emotions is the "post". Abandon hate and anger, they are no use to you. I am watching over you and Beorf. Sartigan will help you to become stronger. Trust him.'

CHAPTER EIGHT

UPSGRAN VILLAGE

rban vanished and Amos woke up with a start. Sartigan had relit the fire and was drinking some tea. It was barely light but Amos noticed that Beorf was already up. He was starving and was wandering in the woods in search of edible roots or berries.

'Your friend is in a very bad mood,' laughed Sartigan. 'He was up before me and has been searching the forest for an hour already. I think he is really hungry…'

'So am I…,' replied Amos, warming himself by the fire. 'We must find something to eat.'

'Yes of course….Not far from here we'll reach the great North Sea. There's a village on the coast where we can get something to eat.'

'Let's set off quickly before Beorf tries to eat a tree!'

'Indeed, wood is so bad for the digestion,' added Sartigan, mockingly.

They loaded up the mule and set off northwards. Beorf really was in a foul temper. He trailed along cursing as he walked. This reaction was typical of the man-bear race whose stomachs dictated their moods. The emptier the stomach, the grumpier the Beorite!

Fortunately the teacher and his two new pupils soon reached the great North Sea and the coastal village of Upsgran. At the side of the road they saw an ancient stone monument on which was carved:

UPSGRAN
103 Inhabitants
Clear Off!

It was obvious that the inhabitants didn't want to be disturbed by strangers. But it was the travellers' only chance of finding something to eat. Beorf simply had to eat and this village might be able to give him back his smile. In any case they needed to buy provisions for the journey as well as some warmer clothing. Even Sartigan, who never seemed to shiver, admitted to feeling uncomfortable in the chill winds off the sea.

Upsgran was just a small village lined with long wooden, windowless houses, each one large enough to house several families. Each house was made of stout wooden planks, its solid frame resembling the hull of an upturned boat. The roofs were covered with turf and the three travellers could see poking through the snow the small tufts of the grass which would grow in the summer. The houses were decorated with carvings of sea monsters and demons.

Amos signalled to Beorf to hide his pointed ears and went up to one of the houses. He found a crack between two planks and peered inside. The main source of light was from a hole in the roof. There was a single room with several beds arranged round it. The house was sparsely furnished; it was easy to see that most of the family's possessions were either hanging on the walls or placed in big open chests. There was a huge fireplace in the middle of the room. In front of the fire was an impressive weaving loom.

It was past midday but the whole village seemed to be fast asleep.

'Well,' said Beorf in desperation, 'Is there anything to eat in there?'

'Yes but all the inhabitants of this house are sleeping like logs!' replied Amos. 'Listen to them snoring!'

'Well let's wake them up then,' – Beorf was becoming impatient. 'We can pay them for their trouble!'

'Look!' cried Amos. 'There's a little fishing harbour down there and I can see a place that might be an inn. Let's go and see if we can eat there and get warmed up!'

As they walked down to the harbour Amos was greatly impressed by the ships moored there. They were very long with a single square sail finely woven in wide blue-and-white stripes. About twenty oars hung from each side of the ships. They were decorated with coloured shields and had striking figureheads in the form of monsters. These magnificent vessels swayed gently to the rise and fall of the waves.

When he reached the inn's door Sartigan stopped.

'There's plenty going on in there! I won't be able to talk to these people. They don't speak my language and I don't have magic ears like you. You go on in and I'll stay here. Good luck, boys and don't get into trouble....I'll keep a look out and wait for you outside.'

Amos and Beorf looked at each other for reassurance. Cautiously, they stepped inside the wooden building. Thick smoke from the fire hung in the air before slowly escaping through a big hole in the ceiling. A ray of sunlight pierced the gloom of the windowless inn. Six brutish looking warriors who had been sitting round a table stood up and stared at Amos and Beorf.

They were obviously tough warriors who took pride in their appearance. Each wore a chainmail coat and rough leather trousers fastened at the calf by a strap. They wore conical metal helmets with nose guards and carried long lances, axes and two-handed swords and round shields. They had thick capes and broad belts. They were strongly built with big bellies, long beards and thick moustaches.

It was clear the two boys had disturbed them in the middle of their meal. On the table were thick slices of buttered bread, roast beef, boiled ham, boars' meat sausages, venison, grilled reindeer and an amazing quantity of wild berries, nuts and vegetables. Beorf had already identified each dish by its smell. His mouth was watering and he prayed that the strangers would invite them to join in their meal.

The largest of the six warriors picked up a jug of water and threw it at the boys as hard as he could, shouting:

'Get out vermin! We don't serve strangers here!'

'I'll serve who I like in my inn!' shouted a fat woman, coming out of the kitchens. 'I make the decisions here!'

The woman was drying a big cast iron frying pan. She stepped up to the unfriendly brute and hit him with it, full in the face. The man fell down, clutching his head.

'If I catch anyone else meddling in my affairs I'll turn his nose into a pancake!' she threatened, brandishing the heavy pan.

The warriors scowled and continued their meal, all the while glaring at the intruders. The woman turned to Amos and Beorf:

'Well young sirs. What are you doing here? You shouldn't be in a place like this!'

'We've come a long way,' said Amos respectfully. 'We have crossed the great forest to the south of your delightful village and we have run out of supplies. Can we eat here? We have the means to pay you!'

'My dear boy!' she said looking scornfully round at her customers, 'if everyone here was as well mannered as you, my life would be much easier. You have a nice southern accent too…I've always liked that…'

'Can we eat then?' asked Beorf anxiously

'Well no…not really…not now anyway…' the fat woman hesitated. 'There's an important meeting going on here so I'll have to ask you to come back later.'

'I'm starving,' bellowed Beorf suddenly. Enraged by the woman's refusal, his arms had turned into paws and his teeth into ferocious fangs.

'Give me some food,' he demanded, 'or I'll help myself!'

Beorf turned to look at the table full of food. He couldn't believe his eyes! The warriors were all smiling at him showing their…bear fangs. They were all Beorites! Even the woman now had rounded ears and thick fur covering her arms. She asked:

'Who are you, young bear, and where are you from?'

'I am called Beorf Bromanson and I am the son of…'

'Evan! Evan Bromanson's son!' she exclaimed excitedly. 'Did you hear that? It's Evan's son!'

The warriors all got up at once and hugged Beorf. They tossed him into the air many times, rubbing his head and laughing happily. Their eyes shone with pride and joy to find one of their kin. The bear-woman cried:

'The Bromansons are back in Upsgran. I'm going to wake the whole village!'

Beorf tried in vain to get a word in edgeways. They grabbed hold of him and he landed on a chair near the table where they bombarded him with questions:

'How are your mother and father?'

'Did Evan get another drakkar?'

'Is your mother still as pretty?'

'Your mother, Hanna, was the prettiest girl in the village! Surely she told you that, didn't she?'

'Evan's a good father isn't he?'

'What are they doing now?'

'Where are they living?'

'Did they talk about us? And about Upsgran?'

'Did Evan ever tell you about the time we fell off the cliff at Ryhiskov together?'

'Always got his nose in a book, your father hasn't he?'

'Did he ever find the answers to his questions?'

'Is he here? Will he come soon?'

All the words, questions and exclamations were jumbled together while Beorf ate! He stuffed himself, laughing. Bread and meat, fruit and honey! Paradise was called Upsgran from now on!

Amos was invited to share the meal. He went out to fetch Sartigan and told him:

'I have good news and bad news, master!'

'Start with the good news,' replied Sartigan with a wide smile.

'We have found friends in the village!' exclaimed Amos.

'And the bad news?' asked the old man intrigued.

'Beorf's diet...there's a slight problem with it!' laughed Amos.

CHAPTER NINE

BANRY BROMANSON AND THE FUNERAL OF EVAN AND HANNA

A heavy silence descended on the inn at Upsgran as Beorf, choked with emotion, recovered enough to tell how his parents had died. The whole village was there. The hundred and three Beorites who made up the community had come out of hibernation to see Bromanson's son and to hear his story. Beorf explained how his father had been captured by the Knights of the Light at Great Bratel. Evan had fought like a true man-bear. He made them pay dearly for his capture. On the orders of Yaune the Purifier, his mother, too, had been imprisoned. His parents were accused of witchcraft and had gone to the stake together. They had died hand in hand, their eyes full of fear but also shining with the love they felt for one another.

It took a few minutes for the assembled company to dry their tears. Upsgran was the village where Evan and

Hanna had been born. Everyone had known, loved and cherished them. One man stood up and took off his horned helmet. He was very tall with long brown hair, a short well-trimmed beard and broad shoulders.

'I am Banry Bromanson,' he said 'head of the great clan of Bromanson and leader of this village. Your father was my brother and the clan is now yours. They call me "The Sea Serpent" because I am more seaman than hunter. If you want to avenge Evan's death I will accompany you even into Hell itself!'

'I am Helmic the Insatiable,' called another man from the back of the room.

Helmic was well built and looked like a warrior. Unlike the other Beorites he was completely bald and had no beard. He had piercing blue eyes, a narrow nose, small ears and a large belly.

'They call me "The Insatiable" because there's never too much for me to eat or drink, or enough battles and adventures for me to enjoy! I've sailed to all four corners of the world already, but I'm ready to set off right now! My house is open to you and your friends.'

'You can count on my support...my word is my bond!' exclaimed two more men in unison.

It was the Azulson brothers. They were both of medium height but the two warriors had completely different faces. One looked sullen and rough, while the other had fine features and looked less robust.

'I'm Goy and he's Kasso,' said the rough-looking one, scowling.

'I can speak for myself!' said the other. 'Please excuse my brother, he has no manners. We were brought up differently. I was raised by my mother and he by our father. My brother is a little, shall we say...basic!'

'Is that right? It's you who's basic, you puny creature!' rasped Goy 'I'll give you manners! Mr Kasso here eats nothing but nuts and grapes in case he puts on weight! He's so useless in combat that I have to do all the work!'

'Why risk my life when I've got you at my side, Goy!' retorted Kasso. 'You act...but I do all the thinking. I'm the brains and you are the muscle. Besides you've never...'

'Shut up!' a deep voice boomed through the throng. 'Those two never stop arguing....'

Another six people stood up, it was those who had first confronted the boys at the inn. The biggest of them, a grizzly bear of a man about two metres tall and weighing about a hundred and fifty kilos, stepped forward. His hair was long and plaited and he had a thick red moustache. He wore an impressive metal helmet decorated with two black crow's wings. He said:

'I am Piotr Bailson – they call me "The Giant of Upsgran"! Allow me to introduce my companions. This is Geser Michson, and he's called "The Stone Marten".

He knows the forest better than anyone. Aldred Girson is "The Axe", and he's the wildest fighter I know. Rutha Bagason's known as "The Valkyrie". She's the only woman in our group, and her exploits are famous all along the north coast. We call Chemil Lapson here "Fairy Fingers", and he's the best carpenter on the continent. And this is Hulot Hulson, known as "Big Mouth". Hulot has seen and done everything but has never been outside the village!'

Everyone burst out laughing, so easing the emotion over the news of Evan's and Hanna's death. Hulot opened his mouth to defend his honour, but quickly closed it again.

'We're the Upsgran guard,' continued Piotr 'The Giant'. 'In winter, we protect our friends as they sleep. We are called "The Crows" and we would be delighted to welcome you into our group. In fact, we could do with some reinforcements and you could learn a lot from us. It would be an honour to command the son of Evan Bromanson, our former clan leader…'

'My father was clan leader?' exclaimed Beorf in astonishment.

'Yes,' said Banry. 'My elder brother was the greatest clan leader this village has ever known. He had a rare strength and courage. He was also very clever and did a great deal for the Beorites of Upsgran. When he left I took his place temporarily. For years we have been waiting for him to return and now you have come in his place.'

'But why did my father leave the village?' asked Beorf, hungrily taking in his uncle's words.

'For a very simple reason. He wanted to find answers to his questions. What he did know, led him to believe that the race of man-bears had become scattered throughout the world and risked extinction. He wanted to go to a city to find people and books to help him understand our people better and perhaps to reunite them.'

'But...can I ask a question?' interrupted Amos. 'Why did Evan think your race would become extinct?'

'Because of the curse!' bellowed Helmic. 'We are an accursed race, that's the truth of it!'

'Don't say that. There's no actual proof!' snapped Piotr.

'I have seen no children in Upsgran,' said Amos. 'Is that normal?'

'No, it is not normal...' admitted Banry. 'For several years our children have all died in infancy. They've barely begun to walk when they are carried off by a strange illness. They suddenly stop breathing in the night. We can do nothing to save them...that's the main reason my brother left the village. He wanted to understand what was happening so that he could help us. He wanted answers and he must have discovered something because Beorf is a Beorite's son and he is...alive! Without children we will die out. We've also had these foul mouthlins prowling around lately…'

'The Red Caps!' cried Beorf. 'Have they been here?'

'They tried to take the village!' laughed Piotr. 'Until we got in their way! They will come back in bigger and more savage hordes, though. That's what we were having a meeting about when you arrived at the inn this morning. I beg your pardon for the way we greeted you. We were worried and…'

'We understand,' said Amos gently.

'Now that our former leader and his beloved wife are dead we owe them a funeral worthy of their rank and of the love we felt for them. We'll speak later of our problems. Tonight, we shall pray that Evan and Hanna, two children of Upsgran, will rest in peace.'

On Banry's orders craftsmen carved two tree trunks into the likenesses of the dead couple. The carvings were then placed in the centre of the village as a memorial to them. The Bromansons' longship was dragged out of the water. All the personal belongings that Evan and Hanna had left behind were placed in the ship. Everyone added some trinket which reminded them of the couple. Carrying a flaming torch, Banry stepped forward and set fire to the longship. As the sun slowly slipped behind the mountains, all the people of Upsgran sang a funeral hymn.

Once the ceremony was over all the villagers moved to the harbour inn where a feast awaited them. All evening long funny stories were told about Evan and compliments were paid to Hanna. As the Beorites were speaking their own language, Sartigan was using Beorf's crystal elf's ears. Like this, he could follow the ceremony well. The pointed ears were carefully hidden under a headband as he rose and began to speak:

'If you will allow me, I should like to tell you a story!'

'Go ahead!' said Helmic the Insatiable, 'I love stories!'

'One day a man lost his horse. The animal ran off and galloped far away from its master. It was a magnificent creature so the man was sad to lose it, but said to himself: "Perhaps this misfortune will bring some good luck." After several months, the horse returned with another equally fine horse. The man now had two magnificent horses, but he said to himself: "Perhaps this good fortune will turn into bad luck." One day the man's son, who loved riding in the meadows, suffered a terrible fall and lost the use of a leg. The man looked at his son, now handicapped for life, and said: "I can't see how any good luck will come from this misfortune!" A year later enemies attacked the kingdom and all the young men were sent to fight. Most of them were killed. But as the man's son was disabled he could not fight and stayed at home with his father. Do you understand the meaning of this story, good people of Upsgran?'

'It means you should never trust a horse!' cried Goy from the back of the room.

'No it doesn't' sneered his brother Kasso. 'Sartigan means that good fortune is never far behind misfortune and that we should trust to our fate. The deaths of Evan and Hanna have brought Beorf to fulfil his destiny among us.'

'I think Kasso is right,' agreed Banry. 'Fate brought you here and that must be for a reason.'

'If you will let me explain,' said Amos. 'We are hunting for the Red Caps and we have discovered that they are robbing towns and villages to gather up a great treasure for a…dragon's lair.'

At the mention of the dragon a great gasp of fear arose from everyone present.

'These Red Caps killed my father and captured my mother. I must find my mother and fight the dragon as best as I can. Sartigan is here to help me and Beorf is my right arm. He is the truest friend that I know…'

'You have said enough young man,' interrupted Piotr the Giant. 'At this very moment, the Vikings north of here are gathering a great army in order to fight this dragon. They sent an ambassador here to Upsgran. King Harald Blueteeth invites us to join his ranks. Beorites have never before got involved in Viking affairs but I think now is the time.'

'I agree,' said Banry. 'It's a tradition for us to offer a token of our allegiance to King Harald. We should give him a large sum of money as our contribution to his war chest.'

'But we haven't a bean!' said Hulot Hulson. 'We'd better forget it! Let's stay where we are....We're better off at home! I'm all for adventures, but a dragon...that's no adventure...its more like suicide!'

'We've got what you need!' said Amos heading for the door. 'Come on, Beorf, you can give them a present.'

The boys went to the stable where the mule was tied and took out the casket of sapphires. They returned to the inn and placed it in the middle of the table before revealing its contents to cries of surprise and admiration.

'This is for the war chest!' said Beorf proudly.

'You are a worthy son of your father,' said Banry to his nephew. 'Helmic, Piotr, Aldred, Rutha, Chemil, Hulot Hulson, Goy and Kasso! Prepare yourselves! In one week, we're off to war!'

'And that dragon better stay in its lair!' yelled Helmic, brandishing his long sword.

CHAPTER TEN

THE NORTH SEA

The preparations for war went well. They chose the sturdiest of the drakkars, one of the longships moored in the harbour, as a warship. It had been entirely reinforced – from the hull to the tip of the mast. The blacksmith attached a metal spike to the prow which could spear smaller vessels or sink them. The women of the village wove a new blood-red sail and the carpenters made longer, sturdier oars. An impressive amount of food was loaded: sausages and smoked meat, roast chickens and big pieces of salt bacon, jars of pickled vegetables, potted meats, cheese, goats' milk, beer, wine, potatoes, beans, buckwheat flour, bread and an astonishing quantity of honey. In addition to the chainmail armour, long lances, axes, shields, helmets, bows and arrows, there were dozens of furs for the freezing nights ahead at sea, changes of clothing, a grindstone to sharpen their weapons, packets of medicinal herbs, navigational instruments, all types of tool, candles, oil lamps, a brazier and firewood.

After a few days the ship looked more like a merchant ship than a warship. The Beorites didn't want to stint themselves while at sea which was why they needed a whole week to get ready. Beorf spent most of his time helping with the preparations.

Amos and Sartigan were making preparations of their own. The old man was beginning to train the young mask wearer both physically and psychologically. He told him many stories, rich in wisdom for those who could learn:

'In my country, a long time ago, a powerful king who had no heirs to succeed to his throne decided to hold a great contest. The first man to light a candle with a single arrow would become the new king. The country's best archers came to try their luck. There were some skilful shots which grazed the candle wick without managing to light it. The king was disheartened. He began to think he would never find someone to succeed him. Just as he was about to call off the contest, a young peasant boy appeared. The boy took an arrow in his right hand and refused the bow that was offered to him. He covered the arrow with soot, set it alight, and walked up to the candle and lit it. The rules of the contest specified that whomsoever lit the candle with a single arrow would become king. The king had not said that you had to use a bow! In real life we sometimes take things at face value, without really understanding the true meaning. You must learn to look beyond appearances….'

Amos enjoyed his new teacher's stories. They were so full of wisdom they made him think and question himself. He began to spend long periods meditating. Sartigan wanted him to concentrate on letting the magic flow through him. Amos needed to keep a cool head at all times; he had to control his emotions and forget his hatred of those who had killed his father in order to act as rationally as possible.

To reinforce his message, Sartigan told him a story about his own teacher. He was a monk, a clever man, but one who spoke very little. This monk and his disciples attended an important archery contest. The best archers in the whole country were there. The monk had no interest or training in the sport, but he won the contest by firing three arrows into the centre of the bull's-eye. Sartigan, who in those days excelled as an archer, found it hard to accept his master's victory. He asked him respectfully what the secret of his success was. The monk told him that all the archers in the tournament were competing with each other and were desperate to win. The pressure of the contest had overwhelmed them. Their eyes darted around anxiously and their hearts pounded. Not only did they want to win but they were terrified of losing! In order to win you must keep your mind and spirit calm. Fear is useless and must be replaced by focus.

'You often speak of "focus", Master Sartigan,' Amos said. 'But what does that mean exactly?'

'It means that you follow your own path!' replied the old man, delighted by the question.

'Yes, but how do you apply that in everyday life?' asked Amos.

'I shall answer you with another question, young man,' replied Sartigan. 'If you had to choose one of the seven colours of the rainbow, which would it be?'

'Could you remind me of the colours, please?' asked Amos.

'Red, orange, yellow, green, blue, indigo and violet.' The teacher reeled them off.

'I think…I think I'd choose the one that I could still see in my mind once the rainbow had disappeared.'

'There you are then!' exclaimed Sartigan proudly. 'You've answered your own question. Focus is what you retain. That is why one must always be learning many things…without ever stopping. No matter what your age, there are thousands of things to learn. Each day we have hundreds of new experiences, and everything we learn increases our understanding! Just as you said, it is the colour that stays with us.'

'Will you still tell me your stories while we are at sea?' asked Amos 'I enjoy them and they give me confidence.'

'I shall not be coming with you,' said Sartigan. 'I shall stay here and wait for you.'

'But I need you!' cried Amos, disappointed. 'You are a dragon-hunter.... You have to come with me. I will never be able to fight a creature like that on my own!'

'You are forgetting what I have taught you already! My role is no longer that of dragon-hunter. I am here to teach you what I know. You must fight alone. I am not the mask wearer, you are....It is your task!'

'But how...how shall I manage without you?'

'Remember the stories I told you about not making assumptions and having no fear of losing. Remember those two things and you will overcome the dragon! I shall wait in the village for your return.'

'And if I...supposing I don't return?' asked Amos hesitantly.

'Then I would die waiting for you,' answered Sartigan, calmly. 'I was freed from the ice to become your teacher and to teach Beorf at the same time. The young manimal is not yet ready for my teaching. On his return he will be. Now then, go and prepare yourself; the Beorites are ready to leave.'

Amos gathered up his few belongings, collected his crystal ears and walked over to the drakkar. The equipment was being loaded. Beorf was bustling about, obeying his uncle Banry's every order. Once everything was stowed for the long voyage, Amos went on board.

'Well, Amos, aren't you excited to be starting?' asked Beorf.

'Yes, but I have been happier!' said the boy bitterly. 'I thought Sartigan was coming with us...'

'What? You mean he's not coming!' cried Beorf'

'No, he says it's for me to face the dragon alone....I thought that because he was a dragon-hunter...well I thought he was coming with us to fight the dragon himself. I keep trying to think like him and tell myself...some good should come of all this!'

'But supposing it all just gets even worse?' said Beorf, sounding worried.

'I don't know....I just don't know any more...,' said Amos with a shrug. 'We'll see....'

In the growing winter cold the drakkar hoisted its big square sail and slipped out of the harbour. Each crew member was seated at an oar. Banry, at the tiller, began a steady chant and the rowers kept time with its rhythm. Beorf and Amos shared a seat and pulled on the same oar. The whole village had gathered on the quays to see the brave warriors leave. The ship was soon out of the bay and into the open sea.

For three consecutive days, the Beorites rowed without eating, without sleeping and without stopping to rest for a moment. Amos remembered Sartigan telling him that manimals had immense stamina and could choose whether to hibernate or not. These Beorite warriors had controlled their appetite. They knew exactly when to exert themselves and when they needed to build themselves up. The drakkar moved ahead at great speed. Mere humans could not have kept up this pace.

Helmic the Insatiable rowed wildly. Great drops of sweat dripped from Aldred the Axe, while Piotr the Giant, an oar in each hand, did the work of two Beorites. Rutha the Valkyrie yielded to no one and sneered at Goy's rowing style. Only Kasso Azulson took no part in the rowing. He looked after the sail, studied the stars and decided which route to follow. As a navigator there was none better and Banry, the captain and helmsman, had total confidence in his right-hand man. Kasso was able to anticipate how the wind would blow and knew the sea currents better than anyone. Chemil Fairy Fingers and Hulot Hulson shared an oar. These two Beorites had never left Upsgran before and were anxious about embarking on this journey. No carpenter could mend boats better than Chemil and no one could outdo Hulot's storytelling. Banry had chosen him so that, on their return, he could recount the great adventure of the Beorites of Upsgran.

After three days of sailing in cold and difficult conditions, with high winds and crashing waves, Kasso shouted:

'Burgman Island in sight!'

'Keep rowing my friends!' cried Banry, changing to a faster chant.

Amos had hardly slept, although he was exhausted by the journey. He had been lying in the hold suffering from seasickness ever since they had set off and had been sick several times. He wanted only one thing: to reach dry land as quickly as possible!

Beorf, on the other hand, was feeling rather well. Even though he was horribly tormented by hunger pangs, he performed like a true Beorite. He hadn't had a bite to eat for three days. He was too young to keep up with the adults and had fallen asleep several times. But he had no problems with seasickness and was a useful member of the crew. As well as taking care of Amos, he had helped Kasso set the sail and kept the rowers supplied with drinks. He had also held the tiller whenever Banry was poring over his sea charts.

The drakkar came to a standstill in one of the bays of Burgman Island. The Beorites quickly hauled the longship up onto the pebbly beach and began to set up camp. They were an amazingly efficient crew with each member knowing exactly what he had to do. In no time at all the big tent was up and a delicious meal was steaming in their mess tins. They consumed a huge quantity of meat. The sound of chewing, accompanied by contented rumblings, filled the air of the little island. Kasso alone did not join in – he ate just nuts and grapes.

After the meal all the Beorites raced into the icy sea for a swim. Beorf hesitated for a long time before joining them but, encouraged by Amos, he found the willpower to overcome his reluctance. This traditional bathing was meant to increase the flow of blood to their aching muscles. The cold water speeded up their heartbeat so that their blood flowed quickly from their fingertips to their heels, helping their aching muscles recover. Although this seemed to be good for Beorites, Amos thought that shock treatment like this after an enormous meal would probably be suicidal for a human! He remained on the beach, laughing at the shouts and jokes of the bathers.

After their swim the crew made themselves comfortable in the tent and slept for two whole days. Amos found it hard to sleep because of the earth-shaking snores of the Beorites. Sometimes he thought that the island was shuddering with a volcanic eruption. He left the tent and lay down to rest under dozens of furs on board the ship. He thought the Beorites sometimes behaved very strangely. There was no middle way for them – it was all or nothing! This probably explained Beorf's unshakeable friendship.

Kasso was the first to wake. He fetched a bucket of icy water and began to splash it onto his fellow crewmen.

'Get up, Beorites!' he cried. 'We've a long way to go! You can hibernate another time! On your feet, you lot of good-for-nothings!'

'Why do you wake them up so roughly?' asked Amos, surprised at this treatment.

'Because they've eaten too much again! If I didn't do this they'd still be snoring two weeks from now! That's why I eat so little…so that I don't sleep too long! Of course I don't use as much energy as they do…I don't do any rowing.'

'I see,' said Amos, 'they are true bears and in winter…'

'In winter, they sleep!' finished Kasso, dousing Helmic. 'Get up you lazy bunch of snails! Shake yourselves! We're about to leave.'

One by one, the Beorites slowly got up. Although they were soaked, they didn't seem to mind being woken like this. Even Banry had an icy shower and with water running down his face, merely said, 'Thanks Kasso, we can always rely on you!'

'No problem!' he replied as he doused his brother, Goy.

'What's going on!' shouted Beorf when it came to his turn for a bucket of water.

'It's nothing, Beorf. Apparently it's the only way to

make you wake up....I shall have to remember that next winter!' laughed Amos.

After an enormous breakfast they set off for the lands of Harald Blueteeth. Amos was feeling better now that his seasickness had subsided. The sea was much calmer too and the drakkar was hardly pitching. The wind had dropped and the sail had been taken down. Banry was singing lustily to give the rowers their rhythm when he suddenly fell silent. The captain stood up from his seat and scanned the horizon in all directions. Solemnly, he turned to face his men and said:

'Merriens...mermen...I can sense them under the water and they've got us surrounded!'

'Leave them to me!' begged Aldred, waving his two-handed sword. 'Please leave them to me!'

'Are we having fish tonight then, Aldred?' asked Rutha. 'Perhaps I'll help you to fillet them!'

'Be quiet!' ordered Banry. 'First, block up your ears with wax! Second, play dead. Wait till I give the order and then you can turn them into pulp! Is that clear?'

'As clear as daylight!' snarled Helmic through gritted teeth. 'Especially the bit about pulp!'

'But what's going on?' said Beorf to Amos, nervously.

'I think we're about to be attacked by mermen,' he answered. 'I remember what Crivannia the mermaid told me about them. Mermen are like mermaids except that they are repulsively ugly. They use their voices to entrap humans. They are sea monsters who devour their victims, steal cargoes and sink ships to make houses for themselves at the bottom of the ocean. I read in Al-Qatrum that they wear red hats with feathers. They must be sea-going cousins of the Red Caps!'

'Why don't you use your collar to summon up a few of the hounds?' asked Beorf before blocking his ears.

'No…I've another idea.

The mask wearer put on his elf's ears and waited patiently, playing dead as Banry had ordered. He had remembered what Gwenfadrilla had told him: that the crystal ears would protect him from magic incantations. All at once he could make out the piercing lament of the mermen. Amid the sounds of the wind and waves arose a sweet melody. A chorus of pure clear voices was softly singing:

Alone in his frail ship,
Across the wide ocean,
Sails the helmsman,
Far above him shine the stars,
From the depths his tomb calls to him.
Forward! His destiny calls him!
Beneath the waves and sky,
He will find us waiting…

With his face turned to the deck of the ship Amos sang:

Rise without fear.
Their time has ended moons ago.
This longship is a coffin.
Which sails to the mist of the gods.

The singing stopped and was suddenly followed by a fearful silence. Then came a voice:

Who are you, brother of the waters?
You who speak our language,
With the accent of humankind.

Amos remembered what Sartigan had taught him and calmly answered:

I am a merman.
I am wounded,
Imprisoned in a net.
I tried to flee,
My mouth torn by their hatred.
I took my revenge and they died.

The voice answered him:

Brother, we come.
We shall come up and devour them.

Then horrible webbed hands with long fingernails gripped the longship's side. Faces appeared on all sides. The biggest merman, probably their leader, slid into the boat. He was indescribably ugly. His enormous mouth was filled with hundreds of pointed fish-like teeth. His body was stinking and covered with fish-like scales. A raised crest ran down the length of his back from the top of his head to the tip of his tail. He had small, piercing eyes, a fishtail instead of legs and thick green seaweed covered his head, shoulders and back. He looked very powerful and carried a weapon which looked like a sea urchin. Perched on the side of his head was a red cap with feathers.

When another merman slithered up to Rutha the Valkyrie, Banry grabbed his long sword and cut off its head. That was the signal! The Beorites now had long claws and sharp teeth. Grabbing hold of a merman, Helmic dragged it out of the water and broke its neck. Piotr the Giant killed five with a single movement while Rutha and Goy stood back to back to try to prevent the drakkar being boarded. Hulot and Chemil hid behind Aldred the Axe, keeping out of harm's way and Kasso climbed to the top of the mast. Beorf turned to Amos and said:

'Couldn't you do one of your tricks right now?'

'Don't worry…I'm working on it!'

The young mask wearer overcame his fear and

concentrated hard. Magically, the Beorites' axes and swords began to glow red. Aldred cried out:

'Our axes! The blades are red hot! The gods are with us!'

Spurred on by this supernatural sign, the Beorites' strength increased tenfold. The mermen tried to board the ship without success. Lances, axes and swords pierced and burned their flesh. Kasso, who was sitting astride the crosspiece of the mast, fired arrow after arrow with the precision of an elf. Helmic used his fearsome claws to gouge the faces of his enemies. Aldred the Axe yelled with joy as he cut off one head after another. The air around them was filled with a nauseating smell of fish. Banry, sword in hand, was enjoying himself now, singing a war song from the olden days. Goy and Rutha stood at the prow of the ship striking out without pity or remorse.

Suddenly, Helmic tripped and fell overboard. Piotr yelled as he swung his sword:

'Bear overboard! Bear overboard! Bear overboard!'

Without a moment's hesitation, Beorf leapt into the water. Amos grabbed a sword and covering its blade in magic fire, he hurled it into the sea. He had to concentrate hard so that the blade would stay hot underwater. His friend stretched out his hand and grabbed the hilt as it plunged beneath the water.

Beorf could see a merman dragging Helmic down into the depths. Helmic was struggling in vain to free himself. With all his strength Beorf flung his sword at the creature. The weapon, with its magic fire, sliced through the water and lodged in the merman's shoulder. It lost its grip on Helmic who struggled desperately to reach the surface, fighting for breath.

On board the longship, the battle continued until Banry, in the thick of the fighting, ordered:

'Let the sail down, Kasso we've got to get away!'

Just then Beorf surfaced with Helmic, and Hulot Hulson finally found the courage to act. Drawing his sword, he wounded the merman in their wake, and helped the two Beorites out of the water. The sail dropped and Banry shouted:

'If the gods really are with us the wind will start to blow and get us out of here!'

Amos closed his eyes and raised his hand to the sky. Instantly a breeze got up. The sail filled a little and slowly the ship began to move. Amos used all his power so that the breeze freshened to a wind and then to a gale. The Beorites rushed to their oars and began to pull hard. In a few minutes the ship had left the battle zone and their enemies far behind.

'They're not following us!' called Kasso from the mast top. 'Look! They're splitting up! We have won this battle, my brothers! We've won!'

'We've won!' shouted all the Beorites together.

The wind suddenly dropped for no apparent reason. Amos was sitting on the deck, breathless and drenched with sweat.

'Nice work, Amos!' said Beorf, admiringly.

'Thanks! You didn't do too badly yourself! What did you think of the burning sword?'

'Brilliant! And you didn't turn the wind into a hurricane!' said the Beorite poking gentle fun at him. 'I think Sartigan's lessons must be working...it's a relief to see that your powers won't always destroy everything in our path!'

'I can control the magic better now, but it's still very hard! It's a bit like having a mad horse galloping inside me....Anyway I'm glad I've made some progress.'

'Get some rest...,' said Beorf, 'We've still got a few more long days' sailing ahead of us.'

'How many?' asked Amos.

'Three more days!' came Banry's deep voice. 'We've got to keep going for three more days....'

CHAPTER ELEVEN

HARALD
BLUETEETH

'**B**ring the Beorites in!' demanded a stern voice. The two huge wooden doors leading to Harald Blueteeth's throne-room opened with a loud grating noise. The Beorites, led by Banry, walked with dignity towards the king. On each side of them hundreds of Vikings crowded in, nervously clutching their weapons and anxious to see the man-bears. Hulot Hulson, known as Big Mouth, stepped in front of Banry and stood in front of the massive throne of silver birch. As was traditional, Hulot began a solemn declaration:

'We, the sons of Upsgran, last of the Beorite villages of the South, have come to aid you in your quest. One of your messengers came into our country seeking our help. We are people of great heart and courage. Though we have little to do with humankind, we have decided to put ourselves under your command! I present to you these brave souls who have faced a thousand and one dangers in order…'

'Shut your mouth, you contemptible bear!' the king interrupted scornfully, his voice oozing disgust. 'Show me what you've brought for the war chest and then I'll see if I want to listen to your twaddle!'

Helmic was about to take his axe and lunge at the rude, ungrateful king, but Aldred held him back, quietly urging him to keep calm. Chemil stepped forward and placed the casket of sapphires at Harald's feet. The king commanded one of his men to open it. When he saw the sparkling stones he sneered:

'I accept your gift with great pleasure, now clear off back to the forest and get lost so I can forget about you!'

'But…,' stammered Hulot, puzzled, 'But…I don't understand! Have we done something to offend you?'

'You got here too late, you stupid bunch of circus animals!' yelled the king in a rage. 'You do understand these words…too late? There is no more war and no more fighting. The Vikings have signed a treaty with the Ancient One in the mountain.'

'But…haven't you been attacked by the Red Caps?'

'The Red Caps and the Merriens are with us now,' announced the king. 'The great Viking army will not destroy the fiery one but will help him in his noble task.'

'And just what is this oh-so-noble task?' demanded Aldred, placing his hand on the hilt of his sword.

'He is going to conquer the world!' replied Harald, as if he thought it an excellent idea. 'That's the way it is. We Vikings know where our best interests lie. Go home, you snivelling little Beorites, and prepare for a visit from the goblins. Hand over everything of value: all your gold, jewels and silver and they might just let you live!'

A great burst of laughter rang through the hall. As the Vikings mocked the man-bears with these insults and scorn, they were slowly moving forward to surround them. It was clear that they did not intend to let the man-bears pass. The Vikings were not going to let them leave. Banry leant towards Beorf and whispered:

'You can see why our people have always kept their distance from humans! If your young magician friend…he is a magician isn't he?'

'Sort of,' agreed Beorf.

'Well, if he's got some way to get us out of here he'd better do it soon, otherwise this will end up in a bloodbath. Once our friends here begin to show their claws…nothing will stop them.'

'You've got to do something!' hissed Beorf to Amos.

The young mask wearer stepped up to the throne. The king quietened the crowd with an imperious gesture. Then he spoke:

'Look, he's not a Beorite. His eyebrows don't meet in the middle and he doesn't have a beard yet! You're human then, wormlet?'

'Do you believe in elves?' asked Amos.

'People say they exist but I've never met one!' answered the king sarcastically. 'Same with fairies! All I ever see are goblins!'

'Well then, feast your eyes!' cried Amos, uncovering his ears.

The crowd drew back. The man-bears looked at one another in disbelief. The trickery seemed to be working beautifully.

'The Beorites have an understanding with the elves,' continued Amos. 'We elves now know our friends from our enemies. As you probably know, our powers are considerable! Allow us to go and I shall not turn my anger on you!'

'An elf!' scoffed Harald. 'And what can you do, you impetuous little rabbit, against a hundred of my men?'

Amos was beginning to lose control again. Harald was a vulgar, sneering, self-satisfied oaf. Amos had loathed him at first sight and his magic, stirred up by hatred, began to gallop through his veins. His stomach felt on fire. The mask wearer struggled to recall his teacher's words and the dream in which his father had warned him against anger.

'Well then, elf!' roared the evil king, 'You haven't answered my question! What can you do against a hundred of my men?'

Amos could hardly breathe. Guessing what might be

about to happen, Beorf warned the Beorites quietly of the mayhem Amos might cause. Once more, Amos could see the flame people dancing before him. A little man made of molten lava twirled around pleading:

'Be our god! Be our Master! Set us free...we are good people, we won't do any harm....Set us free!'

Dazed and drenched in sweat, Amos fell to the ground.

'Well, well!' exclaimed the king. 'Such strength, such power this elf has! He hardly has the strength to stand up yet he threatens me with his power!'

'Set us free!' insisted the little lava man. 'Go on. Be our god and let us serve your hate! Let us serve you! We are good people, good people!'

Amos was trembling. He tried to control himself, but couldn't help thinking about his father's death and his mother's kidnap, about Junos' disappearance and the savagery of the goblins. All these images whirled madly around in his head. He had a desperate urge to destroy this place, this kingdom of cowardly yellow bellies! At the same time, he remembered what Sartigan had taught him. In his delirium, the boy felt that his master was there beside him, repeating his advice:

'Remember, Amos, a rain shower does the earth good but a hurricane destroys everything, leaving only chaos. You are the rain, not the hurricane!'

'Set us free, master! Go on!' cried the little lava man. 'Do it!'

'Off with his head!' ordered Harald. 'I've always dreamed of having an elf's head on display.'

One of the Vikings stepped from the crowd, raising his axe to carry out the king's command. The Beorites moved to intervene. Amos regained his self- control just as the situation was about to turn bloody.

The boy stood and pointed his finger at his executioner. A ball of flame struck him full in the face setting fire to his beard and hair. A gasp of surprise rose in the hall. No one dared move. All eyes were fixed on Amos as they watched his magic at work. Then a great gust of wind burst open the throne-room's massive doors and raged around the room. The mask-wearer made the wind swirl around him like a whirlwind till his feet gradually left the ground. Amos was levitating. Waterspouts poured into the room. No one knew where the flood had come from, but it poured unhindered through the big open doors. With it came hundreds of Kelpies, sea creatures with the back legs and head of a fine horse and the torso and arms of a human. They had tails and manes and three fingers on each hand. Walking rapidly across the water they came and stood between the Vikings and the Beorites. Amos, who was still levitating, seemed to be in a trance. He stared at the ceiling of the throne-room without moving, his arms outstretched with the wind supporting him.

Then, when all the Kelpies had taken up their

positions, he said to the king in a strange voice that was no longer his own:

'I am your god, Manannan Mac Lir! Do you remember me Harald Blueteeth? I am the one you have long forgotten! It is I who helped you gain your throne but received no prayers of gratitude. I am the one you betrayed by your dealings with the dragon. I am the one you mock by your treaties with the Merriens. I am the one who has had enough of you! Do you recognise me?'

King Harald was paralysed with fear and could only stammer incoherently.

'You coward!' rasped Manannan Mac Lir. 'Listen to what I tell you, then carry out my orders to the letter. Tomorrow you will break off all dealings with my enemies and you will welcome the Beorites as they deserve. They will bring you a casket full of magic sapphires. One of your most trusted men must take it to your forge and lock the door. A guard must be posted at the entrance so that no mortal can approach. This is your last chance to return to the proper path! You will do as I say or you will feel my wrath! Now!'

Harald opened his eyes abruptly. He was in his own bed and the sun was just rising over the horizon. The king bellowed:

'Guard! Guard!'

'What is it, Your Majesty?' asked the guard as he rushed into the room.

'Tell the chief army officers to come immediately!' ordered Harald. 'I want my chief privy counsellor to cancel all treaties with the armies of the dragon! Tell them to prepare a feast for a grand reception and send a large fleet to welcome a longship from the South! And…and stop staring at me like that and help me get dressed!'

CHAPTER TWELVE

THE NEW HARALD

'Show the Beorites in!' called a welcoming voice. The two huge wooden doors leading to Harald Blueteeth's throne-room were thrown open with great ceremony. An enormous blue and green carpet bearing the symbols of the god Manannan Mac Lir covered the floor. The Beorites, led by Banry, walked with dignity towards the king. On each side of them hundreds of Vikings had crowded in, anxious to greet the new arrivals. Hulot Hulson, known as Big Mouth, stepped in front of Banry and stood in front of the massive throne of silver birch. As was traditional, Hulot began a solemn declaration:

'We, the sons of Upsgran, last of the Beorite villages of the South, have come to aid you in your quest. One of your messengers came into our country seeking our help. We are people of great heart and courage. Though we have little to do with humankind, we have decided to put ourselves under your command! I present to you the brave souls who have faced a thousand and one dangers in order...'

'Yes, yes, my Beorite friend!' cried the king warmly. 'But first you must allow me to tell you that you and your comrades are most welcome here.'

'We thank you with all our heart,' continued Hulot, pleased to have made such a good impression on the king. 'I must tell you, great sovereign, that I myself was almost killed saving two of my party from the claws of Merriens and that without my courage, we would never have reached here.'

The Beorites all began clearing their throats and coughing, urging Hulot to get on with it. Hulot continued:

'Well now...that's enough about my deeds, let's get to down to business! I have here our contribution to your war chest!'

Chemil came forward and placed the open casket full of blue sapphires at the king's feet. Harald gave orders to one of his most trusted men:

'Let this be locked in the forge at once. I thank you most kindly, my friends!'

'It is we who must thank you,' replied Hulot. 'Both the fleet you sent to welcome us and your generous hospitality are greatly appreciated. The feast that greeted us in your great hall overwhelmed us. We were ravenously hungry and the food has put new life into us!'

'I am very pleased to hear that, my brothers!'

exclaimed the king. 'My cooks did say that you greatly honoured them by eating like…like…like true warriors! Since this morning there have been a great many changes in my kingdom which most fortunately coincide with your arrival. I prefer not to explain why, but dozens of Red Caps have moved onto my lands. Will you help me get rid of them?'

'Let us have one of your divisions, and in a week your land will be rid of this infestation!' asserted Banry, stepping forward a pace.

'Banry needs a week because he works so slowly,' said Helmic, laughing. 'In three days I could cut off all their heads!'

'Your enthusiasm will surely inspire my men!' responded Harald Blueteeth with satisfaction. 'They've had little to do of late. We shall discuss our strategy with my military advisor later, but meantime I should like to speak with the young elf…alone.'

'There's no elf with us, great king,' answered Hulot. 'You must have been misinformed!'

'Oh yes there is…,' mumbled the king, 'there is definitely an elf with you. There he is! That boy! I recognise him. I've seen him before…'

All eyes turned to Amos. The mask wearer stepped up to the king and bowed respectfully.

'I am afraid I must tell you that I'm not an elf but a human,' declared Amos.

'But you are a...I...In any case can I talk to you alone, master elf?' asked the disconcerted king.

'With pleasure!'

'My dear friends,' Harald continued. 'My men will show you to your quarters. Get some rest. Make yourselves at home here. We will speak again of our plans for the goblins in a few days time. For the moment I shall detain this young man only and I should like some privacy...'

The Beorites, pleased at the way they had been welcomed, quickly left the throne-room. The Viking onlookers followed them and soon Harald Blueteeth was alone with Amos.

'Is everything to your satisfaction?' asked the king kneeling before the boy.

'Er, yes. Why do you ask?' stammered Amos.

'I know that you have been sent by Manannan Mac Lir and you must know that I have been obedient to our master's orders. There is no longer any treaty with the dragon. I know now which side I am on: my men will fight for you.'

'That's...very good,' answered Amos without understanding a word the king was saying.

'The prophecy was true then!' said the king, returning to his throne.

'What prophecy?'

'This morning, I...I had a dream. Well, you know all

about it. You were there, in my dream! When I woke, I consulted with a high priest in order to read the book of the Ragnarök.'

'What book?'

'You don't know!' cried Harald Blueteeth in astonishment. 'Ah I see... you're testing me....That's all right...I'm ready. The Ragnarök is a chapter in the great book about the creation and destruction of the world. It tells that a terrible evil will be born on Earth. A foul, indestructible serpent which spits fire will spread its poison throughout mankind. The gods will fall into chaos and the world will descend into the worst of times. Foul beasts will engulf and enslave humankind. There will be no sun and no moon, no more day, no more night. Everywhere will be in total blackness with no light. However, it is also written that a young elf, a superior being chosen by the gods, will come back from the land of the dead. He will come to our land to fight the beast. He will be accompanied by a magnificent warrior who will destroy the creature in mid-flight with a single blow from his sword.'

'I don't think that I am the one you've been waiting for!' said Amos, pensively.

Yes you are!' cried Harald. 'Don't play games with me, stop this pretence! I know you are an elf. I saw you in my dream and...well, if it isn't you...my people have no hope!'

'Why is that?'

'Why?' exclaimed the king. 'Because the Red Caps are breeding like rabbits. They are everywhere! They are destroying and pillaging my villages, they attack the coast and are even making raids inland! Soon, the Merriens will have sunk all my drakkars and I'll be defenceless! That's Why! And with all due respect, a dozen Beorites aren't going to change anything.'

'And what if I were that elf?' asked Amos seriously.

'Then we might be able to believe that victory is possible!' declared the king. 'If the Vikings cannot control the evil in their land, I don't see how the dragon can be stopped from spreading itself over the whole world.'

Amos remembered Sartigan's story. The one in which a wise man had won the archery contest. The monk had said that he won because his opponents were frightened of losing. In order to win he had kept both his heart and mind calm. Reassured by these thoughts, Amos brought out his crystal ears and slipped them on. He showed them to the king and announced:

'You can tell your men that the elf in the legend is here! Tell them to take heart once more. Tell them they need no longer be afraid. The Ragnarök prophecy is fulfilled!'

'I knew it!' cried the king. 'I should never have lost faith and let those monsters have their way. A new day has dawned. Come with me, I must show you something.'

Harald and Amos made their way to the king's forge. Behind a big door guarded by a soldier, the boy could hear the sound of violent hammering.

Harald told him: 'Just as Manannan Mac Lir ordered, I had the sapphires taken to the forge as soon as the Beorites gave them to me.'

'But...precious stones cannot be smelted!' cried the astonished boy.

'Exactly!' agreed the king. 'But I was hoping you would be able to tell me what is going on in the forge.'

'I don't know...you must ask your blacksmith.'

'My blacksmith is not here and no one has entered the forge since my most trusted man put the stones in there. One of my men came to tell me about this strange noise while the Beorites were leaving my throne-room. You really don't know what's going on?'

'I have no idea!' Amos assured him as they watched the forge doors shudder with the impact of the hammering.

CHAPTER THIRTEEN

THE NEW MASK

As usual the Beorites slept for two whole days and, as before, the difficult business of waking them fell to Kasso. Amos told Beorf about his conversation with Harald and all the details of the prophecy. He realised that, from now on, he would be obliged to wear his elf ears at all times. He also told him about the noises inside the forge. The hammering had gone on relentlessly for forty-eight hours. Following the instructions he had been given in his dream, Harald had forbidden any one to enter the forge. Just as Amos had finished his story, a Viking from the king's bodyguard came looking for him.

'I'm sorry to disturb you Master Elf, but you're wanted at the forge. Apparently it's urgent!'

The two friends set out immediately. Harald, impatient and nervous, was pacing up and down the corridor. He rushed to meet Amos.

'Whatever is locked behind this door is roaring very fiercely! Can you please do something, because it isn't in a very good mood.'

A horrible cry rang out. The guards jumped and stepped back. Only Amos, with his magic ears, could understand it.

'Don't worry. There's no danger!' he said to reassure the Vikings. 'It's me he wants – the creature is asking for me. I will go into the forge.'

'Do you want me to come with you?' asked Beorf.

'No thanks, but please keep watch,' answered Amos, a little anxiously. 'Anything could happen!'

Amos opened the forge door and went in cautiously. A creature was standing in the shadows, a few feet from the anvil. It was two metres tall and had the head and hind legs of a horse. Its chest and arms were human and it stood on its hind legs, but it had the long mane and tail of a thoroughbred. Inside the forge a strange conversation began, consisting of odd sounds and movements:

'You sent for me,' Amos whinnied. 'Here I am; speak to me!'

'I am pleased to learn that you speak Kelpie,' replied the sea horse creature in his own language. 'Few humans know it.'

'I know your language but not your customs,' said Amos, snorting and pawing the ground. 'How do I pay my respects to you?'

'Snorting like that, is a mark of great respect among our people, especially from one who has no mane.' the Kelpie assured him, pawing the ground.

'What can I do for you?' asked Amos gently tossing his head two or three times.

'I have come to give you something!' replied the creature, giving a kick of his hoof.

'Your gift will be received with gratitude!' the boy assured him, drawing back his lips and showing his teeth.

'You rescued a priest of Manannan Mac Lir,' whinnied the Kelpie lowering his head. 'He has asked me to make this for you to show his gratitude!'

The Kelpie held out his hand and gave Amos a magnificent, translucent blue mask. It was made from hundreds of sapphires and was shaped like a fish's head. The scales overlapped one another. There were four holes in the mask, two on either side of the gills, ready for the Jewels of Power to be placed in them. The mask, an amazingly beautiful object, had been made by the finest of craftsmen. It was very light but immensely strong and around the edges it was decorated with beautiful engravings of starfish and sea anemones, corals and seaweed.

'It is magnificent!' whinnied Amos, shaking his head wildly.

'Thank you!' replied the Kelpie, stamping his hooves on the wooden floor. 'You have earned it!'

'I must insert a Jewel of Power before I put it on,' said Amos, blowing noisily through his nostrils. 'Do you know where I might find such a jewel?'

'We have had most of our riches stolen by Merriens,' explained the Kelpie, with a kick of its back legs. 'You will find what you seek among the dragon's treasure...the jewel belongs to you!'

'I shall take it and I will do my best to be worthy of the power of the mask,' replied the boy, rearing up suddenly.

'Will you help me to get out of here and back to the sea?' asked the Kelpie, shaking its luxuriant mane. 'If the Vikings see me they would be afraid and try to kill me. They don't yet know that we are fighting on the same side.'

'Of course!' said Amos, pawing the ground once more with his hoof.

He threw a large cover over the creature. As he opened the forge door, he saw Beorf smiling and looking at him curiously.

'What on earth was that language you were speaking?' Beorf asked. 'You were prancing and whinnying like a horse. I couldn't help looking through the crack in the door. Did you realise you kept on slobbering?'

'You would have understood if you'd put on your crystal ears!' said Amos, with a smile.

'Ask the king to take his men away. I must take my

friend here back to the sea and no one must see him.'

'I'll take care of that!' said Beorf. 'Stay here, I'll come back to get you!'

A few minutes later, Amos led the Kelpie from the forge to a small cart covered with a tarpaulin. Beorf had arranged everything. The two friends set off towards a beach a little way from the town. There the creature came out of hiding, said goodbye to Amos and Beorf and galloped down to the water before disappearing into the waves.

'What kind of creature was that, exactly?' asked Beorf in astonishment.

'It was a Kelpie,' answered Amos. 'They are kind and extremely polite. Look at the mask he made for me!'

'It's magnificent!'

'All I have to do now… is to find the Jewel of Power among the dragon's treasure!' said Amos with a nervous little laugh.

The Beorites rolled a huge barrel down from the longship. Banry made sure no one was looking while Chemil, armed with his carpenter's tools, cautiously opened the barrel. Amos and Beorf watched and wondered what would emerge from it. To their astonishment, there was another Beorite fast asleep inside. Banry said:

'Piotr the Giant introduced him to you at the inn. It's Geser Michson the Stone Marten. He hates the sea but he has no equal on land.'

'But how did he survive in that barrel?' asked Amos.

'Hibernation, that's the secret!' cried Kasso, preparing to douse him with cold water.

'Yes, that's it...' continued Banry. 'Before we set off, he ate for three days solid then went to sleep in the barrel. Chemil sealed it up carefully leaving a few holes so he could breathe. He's been asleep all the time we've been travelling!'

'Why are you waking him now?' asked Amos as he watched Geser struggling to open one eye.

'Because we need him,' replied Helmic the Insatiable. 'We're going to send him out to spy for us. He is a wonder in the forest. He can make himself invisible to his enemies and he can survive in tough conditions. The Stone Marten will be able to tell us the exact position, movements and numbers of the Red Caps.

'It will be better for us to go up through the forest rather than following the river in search of the dragon,' added Aldred the Axe. 'Vikings are sailors, so the goblins will be keeping an eye on the water.

'And I'll ask Geser to see whether the Red Caps have any prisoners,' said Rutha Bagason, stroking Amos' hair kindly. 'We're here to find your mother as well...'

'Oh, thank you,' cried Amos, touched. 'I often think

of her and wonder what has become of her. I don't know what those goblins might do to her.'

Geser the Stone Marten had woken up and extricated himself from the barrel. Following his friends' instructions, he turned himself into a bear and disappeared into the great northern forest for nearly a week. When he returned he drew a precise map showing the position of the Red Caps, the routes they took and, most importantly, the location of their prison camp. Banry rubbed his hands with great satisfaction, congratulated the Stone Marten and said:

'I know some goblins who are going to be very surprised to see us!'

CHAPTER FOURTEEN

BRISING

rising was a sweet little eight-year-old girl with golden hair and blue eyes. She lived with her family in the little village of Ramusberget at the foot of the great northern mountain. Brising's mother, who was expecting another child, stayed home and took care of the house. Like most men in the hamlet, her father was a woodcutter. Twice a year, the Vikings sailed in to buy all their wood as the Ramusberget trees were of very high quality and could be made into strong, long-lasting drakkars. The whole village depended on this trade for its income and had done so for hundreds of years.

Brising had an elder brother who liked teasing her but one day he had gone too far! He had stolen her favourite doll and hidden it in the forest behind their house. That afternoon as she went to fetch wood for the fire, Brising entered the forest to search for her doll.

Soon she was completely lost. The villagers organised a search at once, but Baron Samedi found her first. The Baron, an ancient god who could take on many shapes, had appeared in the forest that day in the guise of a man: a tall, lanky man as thin as a skeleton. He had bronze-coloured skin and his eyes glowed like burning coals. He wore a top hat, a long, black leather coat and carried a cane with a golden knob in the shape of a dragon's head. It was autumn and the wolves were howling. Brising shivered, but she was not afraid of this strange looking man and quickly snuggled up on his lap. The Baron put his arm around her reassuringly and took a red draconite from his pocket. He thrust the stone roughly into the child's mouth and the draconite set itself into the back of her throat. The Baron then told her this story:

'Long ago the Earth was inhabited by magnificent dragons. For many centuries these huge, powerful creatures who slept on enormous treasure troves in the heart of the mountains were the masters of the whole world. In time, mankind's greed forced them off the face of the Earth. But soon the great race of dragons will be reborn to spread throughout the world again and I have chosen you to be the first! I had pinned my hopes on another little girl, but she turned against me. You will do very well instead!'

Baron Samedi was the god of the dragon race, known also as the Ancients. He had succeeded in secretly forging three draconites. These were precious stones that had to be set into the bodies of three little girls in order to turn them into magnificent dragons. These dragons would lay their eggs in nests of gold and, in a few short years, would spread over every continent to become the world's dominant race. At least this had been the Baron's vision, but all had not gone according to plan.

His attempt to turn Lolya, the young queen of the Morgorian tribe, into a fearsome dragon, had failed. Amos Daragon had taken the draconite from her and placed it in his Mask of Fire. The second stone had been stolen by a lesser god, but the third, now placed in Brising's body, would finally enable him to carry out his plan.

Soon, a great golden dragon was born under the mountain of Ramusberget. The draconite had worked fast: Brising, as her family had known her, had disappeared, in her place was the golden dragon. Baron Samedi changed her name to Ragnarök, meaning 'Twilight of the Gods'. Great changes were to take place in the world. From now on there would be only be one god and only one ruling race – the dragons.

The Baron had allied himself with Thokk, an ice goddess with a heart of stone, who would gather an enormous army of goblins and Merriens to enslave the world. She ruled over the goblins and called them together at the foot of the Ramusberget mountain to join forces with Baron Samedi. She ordered them to loot the towns and villages along the coast and inland to gather treasure for the dragon.

Meanwhile the golden dragon hollowed out a hiding place for herself in the heart of the mountain. As the creature gnawed and dug, the earth shuddered for miles around. The constant growling and rumbling from the mountain alerted those people who lived nearby. Once she had finished making her den Ragnarök burned down the villages which surrounded it. Those who had not had the sense to leave in time did not escape alive. The dragon showed no mercy to her former family, killing her father and brother with great savagery. Her mother was killed with a single bite and died knowing that the child she carried would never see the light of day.

Baron Samedi laughed sadistically, the prophecy was about to be fulfilled and the world would soon be under the power of the dragons.

The Red Caps began to pour sackfuls of gold, silver, jewels and other precious objects into the dragon's lair. The Ancients' treasure grew bigger with each passing day. In the middle of the huge cavern lay Ragnarök. That morning the dragon had flown far to escape the bitter cold of the everlasting snows of the North.

Baron Samedi was pacing up and down in front of the slumped and weary dragon. He was deep in thought and looking worried. The dragon growled sleepily 'The world has no chance against me; I'm the ruler of the Earth from now on!'

'Don't make the mistake I made,' warned the Baron.

'Do you mean that young boy?' asked the huge creature, making herself comfortable on the pile of treasure. 'Are you worried about him?'

'Yes, it's him I'm thinking about,' agreed Samedi. 'He is unpredictable. That boy managed to foil all Seth's plans and carried off Kur, my beautiful dragon.'

'He is no match for me, I am too powerful!' Ragnarök reassured him in her booming voice. 'In a few weeks the Red Caps will have brought enough treasure for me to lay my first eggs. My children will set off all over the country to make their nests. My grandchildren will travel further still bringing chaos to the whole world.'

'And I,' continued Baron Samedi, 'I shall be the supreme ruler of the gods. All thanks to you, my beautiful little Brising!'

'Whom do you speak of?' asked the Ancient, intrigued by the name.

'I meant Ragnarök,' the Baron corrected himself. 'Forget what I just said, my beautiful Ragnarök. Anyway, I don't want Amos Daragon to come anywhere near you...'

'Baron Samedi,' roared the dragon angrily, 'You are my father and I owe you my life, but don't insult me in my own lair! I am a dragon and he is a mere child! How can he be my equal?'

'He is cunning...unbelievably cunning...'

'Go! Leave my mountain, unworthy father!' bellowed Ragnarok. 'You have no faith in me. You think I am too stupid to confront a child! I despise you! What kind of god creates a dragon only to fuss like a nursemaid...I shall prove the greatness of my power to you...I'll make Amos Daragon come here and I'll destroy him with one bite.'

'No, Ragnarök! You mustn't!' cried the baron in alarm. 'He must not come here! Is that quite clear? I cannot take any more risks. The wars between the gods of good and evil have left them exhausted. They are weaker and less vigilant. They all think I have disappeared into oblivion. Now is the time for me to strike and conquer the world! I am not on the side of either good or evil, I work for myself alone!'

'Enough! Get out now!' ordered the dragon. 'You will be master of the heavens and I shall be master of the Earth. Your talk irritates me and I care nothing for the wars of the gods. I am queen here and I don't take orders! I want to see the boy and I want to kill him. It shall be as I decree.'

'Don't make any mistakes when you open your jaws

to bite him!' advised the Baron as he turned to go. 'I shall be watching you to see what you do. The race of the Ancients must be reborn…'

'And it will be reborn!' roared the furious creature.

CHAPTER FIFTEEN

THE JOURNEY TO RAMUSBERGET MOUNTAIN

Harald Blueteeth, Ourm Redsnake and Wasaly of Greenland had laid their plans. The three Viking kings had organised their troops to attack and destroy the goblins and mermen. Ourm Redsnake, who had a powerful fleet of drakkars, was to scour the high seas and eliminate the mermen. Wasaly of Greenland swore to clear the southern Viking territories and to pursue the Red Caps across the mainland. The mountain and its dragon were left to Harald Blueteeth and his men because his army was the biggest and best organised. His men were fierce and fearless and his kingdom produced excellent swords and armour.

King Harald Blueteeth divided his army into six battalions, each commanded by one or more of the Beorites. Banry commanded two hundred men while Helmic had three hundred. The brothers Goy and Kasso

Azulson were in charge of a battalion of scouts, consisting of some fifty archers who could deploy quickly. Rutha the Valkyrie, Aldred the Axe and Piotr the Giant shared almost four hundred warriors between them. Chemil Lapson, the skilled carpenter, stayed behind to supervise the building of fortifications in case the town came under attack. Geser went back to sleep in his barrel, but Hulot Hulson was nowhere to be seen when the tasks were allocated. They searched the town for some time before finding him sheepishly hiding in a drakkar, planning his escape back to Upsgran. He was put in charge of thirty-five men with the task of freeing the prisoners in the Red Caps' camp. Amos and Beorf offered to help and it was decided that they should go with Hulot.

Each battalion was given extremely precise orders. Following a route devised in accordance with Geser the Stone Marten's report, each one was to go back up the mountain forcing the goblins to retreat north. As the snow already lay thick in the forests, the warriors were to use skis. Vikings and Beorites alike were well used to this method of travel and could cover great distances with little effort. The snow and ice gave them a considerable advantage. A rendezvous was arranged where they would all join forces for the final assault on the dragon's mountain.

Only Harald's personal bodyguard of fifty men remained behind to protect the town if it came under attack. The Beorites wished each other good luck. With great dignity each took charge of his battalion and soon the town was empty. As they were about to leave, Hulot vanished again. It was Amos who found his new hiding place. He had taken refuge in the king's prison and double-locked the doors. The poor Beorite was scared to death at the thought of going off to battle.

'Hulot,' cried Amos, 'What are you doing in there? It's time to go!'

'I'm not going…,' he mumbled from behind bars. 'I'm in charge of these men and I say we should stay here for a…and then I'll decide what to do….I'll work out…something or other!'

'What's wrong, Hulot?' asked Amos kindly. 'Are you frightened?'

'Yes,' confessed Hulot, collapsing onto the bench of his cell. 'I am so scared that I locked myself in here. I was born fearful and have no gift for fighting. All I'm good at is storytelling. I can use my tongue well enough but I am no leader of men.'

'What is your favourite story?'

'The story of Sigurd! He's the most famous hero I know. He was the one who defeated the great dragon, Fafner, hundreds of years ago. Fafner was once a man, a great magician's son. Then he killed his father and was changed into a dragon because of his greed. Many heroes came in search of the fabulous treasure he kept in his lair, hoping for fame and riches. Many died alongside his lair, but young Sigurd, armed with his father's sword, managed to defeat the monster. He hid in a hole on a path that the dragon used every day and plunged his sword into its belly and killed him.'

'A new legend is being written right now,' said Amos, weighing his words carefully.

'But we shall all die if we attack the dragon! I don't want to die. I want to see Upsgran again,' said Hulot despairingly.

'Someone once told me that you have to replace fear with knowledge. Your story has given me an idea….We need more than strength to fight a dragon. It's no good attacking with armies, we need to attack its weak spot.'

'Do you know how to get rid of a dragon?' asked Hulot timidly.

'Yes! It will take great cunning and at the same time I shall be helping someone we met called Augure De VerBouc!'

'Well…you have convinced me, Amos. I'm coming with you! Let's get those prisoners free….Tell the men we're on our way!'

'Come out then and let's get moving. We've no time to lose!'

'It's just that…oh, dear…I've…um…swallowed the key to the cell!' stammered the Beorite. 'I'll have to wait until nature takes its course to get it back.'

'We'll wait…,' laughed Amos. 'We'll wait!'

Hulot's battalion skied for half a day until they came to the place on the map where the Red Caps' camp was indicated. There, the goblins had taken over an area of flat land. In the middle of the camp were big wooden cages each holding dozens of prisoners waiting to be sold into slavery. The goblins had built makeshift walls of snow all around the camp to keep out the wind. Five huge fires burned day and night filling the surrounding forest with smoke. Red Caps marched up and down keeping watch over the area.

'Do you have a plan?' Beorf asked his friend Amos.

'Hmm. Just make sure Hulot doesn't give any orders yet. I'm going to have a look around!'

Amos concentrated hard and held out his hand. A little blue tit landed on his finger and he spoke softly to it:

'Let me see with your eyes, little friend. I have the power of the wind and I will not harm you.'

The blue tit flew off towards the camp and landed on one of the wooden cages. Through the bird's eyes Amos could see the desperation of the prisoners. They were mostly women and children, but there were also a few men. They looked very weak and ill, huddled together, shivering with cold. The children were covered with filthy torn blankets. The only food was raw fish and some dry bread. The bird took flight again and Amos now saw a familiar figure. A tall, well-built man was helping a weeping woman put another blanket over her sick child. The blue tit perched nearby and Amos instantly recognised Junos, the ruler of Berrion. Fantastic! Was his mother Frilla being held there too?

The blue tit landed on Junos' shoulder. Surprised that a wild bird should do this, the knight stroked its head gently with his forefinger. The bird flew off and Amos lost sight of his friend. He turned and saw that Beorf was already back.

'Junos is with the prisoners!' he cried.

'Have you seen him? What about your mother?'

'I didn't see her but I hope she's there, too. I will roast those goblins alive for what they've done…'

'You're getting carried away again Amos!' said Beorf, trying to calm his friend. 'When you let your emotions get the better of you, you are a danger to everyone.'

'You're right…but we've got to do something!'

'Leave that to me!' said Beorf, confidently. 'I've got a plan…'

'I trust you, Beorf,' said Amos, squeezing his friend's arm. 'I'll leave you to get on with it!'

Beorf and Hulot had made themselves look as monstrous as possible: half man, half bear, they looked more like trolls than human beings, with their twisted mouths and bodies partly covered with fur. Beorf had put on his crystal ears so that he could talk to the goblins. To make themselves look like slave traders they led in a dozen Viking prisoners, all with weapons well hidden under their clothes. Amos was among them, head bowed and tied up like the others. The remainder of the battalion waited in the woods ready to attack.

When the bedraggled band reached the Red Caps' camp, a guard stepped in front of Beorf and demanded:

'Who you are? You telling me or me killing you!'

'Calling me, Guerk!' replied the young manimal. 'Father and me having slaves. Father not talking, not having tongue, humans cutting out!'

'We not paying slaves, we taking from villages!' answered the goblin.

'We paying good price for strong men…,' continued Beorf.

'You coming in. Seeing chief,' said the Red Cap letting everyone come in.

Amos slipped away from the others and approached Junos' cage. The knight stared at him in astonishment, as if he were seeing a ghost.

'Amos!' he murmured. 'I can't believe it! What are you doing here?'

'I'll tell you later if you don't mind,' said the boy, glancing round to see if he had been spotted. 'Is my mother here?'

'No, I'm afraid not.' said Junos sadly. 'They sold her in a slave market two weeks ago. I haven't seen your father, Urban. Did he manage to escape?'

'My father was killed during the attack on Berrion.'

'I'm so sorry…' whispered the knight, his voice choked with emotion. 'He was such a good man…I hope he died….'

'I know.' Amos interrupted him. 'We'll talk later, Junos. Take these weapons and give them to the other prisoners. When Beorf gives the signal we shall attack!'

'Right. Pass them to me. I'll take care of everything. If you can just open the cage doors….These prisoners will gladly fight for you. Even the women will be ready to cut a few goblin throats.'

One by one, each Viking surreptitiously passed weapons to the captives. The goblins were too busy looking at the two strange creatures leading the group to notice anything else. Meantime the goblins' leader came to meet Beorf. He was bigger than the others and sported a feather in his cap. He spoke in a superior tone:

'What you wanting with me and us?'

'Me bringing slaves to you. Not costing much,' answered Beorf politely in his monster guise.

'But…you mad!' cried the chief. 'Me not buying, me selling slaves! Me not needing you slaves!'

'We very sorry great chief,' apologised Beorf. His plan was working a treat. 'We sorry disturbing you. Father and me giving you slaves, saying we sorry you!'

'Present, hmm! For that me not killing you. Only keeping you our slaves!'

All the goblins burst into sinister laughter. Beorf, too, pretended to laugh cheerfully. The chief looked surprised:

'You not understanding me! Me telling you, you being my slaves. Me taking your slaves and keeping you slaves too! No laughing; crying you!'

'Me laughing because you too stupid' said Beorf. 'You falling my trap, great donkey, you!'

The fat goblin was so stunned he didn't react.

'Attack!' yelled Beorf.

The Vikings gave a great shout as they pulled out their weapons. Beorf turned into a bear and leapt at the goblin leader's face. Hulot launched himself into the fray like a wild thing, his fear, at last, forgotten in the heat of battle. The cage doors were quickly flung open to free the prisoners who were thirsting for revenge. Happy to find a sword in his hand once more, Junos gave free rein to his rage. Few of the goblins fought back as the battle quickly spread through the camp. Most of them offered little resistance and several ran off into the forest. Very soon Hulot's men cried victory.

Beorf and Junos embraced each other and once the two boys had introduced Hulot and the Vikings to their old friend, it was agreed that the battalion should escort the freed captives back to the town as quickly as possible. They needed food and warmth and many needed urgent care.

Makeshift stretchers were made and the battalion, with Hulot at its head, was ready to set off. It was then that Amos and Beorf announced that they were going on alone.

'Come back with us,' begged Junos. 'It will be dangerous and I don't want to lose you again!'

'I have no choice,' said Amos. 'I've got to get to Ramusberget mountain as soon as possible. Tell me Junos, was my mother well when you last saw her?'

'Yes,' the knight assured him. 'But she was very worried about you and your father. She never stopped talking and worrying about you both. Poor Frilla. It will be a terrible shock when she hears about Urban.'

'That's if I ever manage to find her,' sighed Amos.

'Don't lose faith, my dear friend! After all, you found me. Nothing's impossible! Look after yourselves! We'll meet again soon!'

'Goodbye, Junos!' said the boys in unison.

They fastened on their skis and set off northwards, carrying a copy of Geser's map. Beorf reckoned that they should reach the mountain within five days.

CHAPTER SIXTEEN

BRISING'S DOLL

A mos had skied before, but he had never travelled so far and so fast. By nightfall his legs and arms ached terribly and each morning he found it harder to straighten up again. Beorf always took a snow bath after supper having learnt from the Beorites that it was the best way to cope with aching muscles. Luckily the sun had shone for the whole journey. There had been no snowstorms and the nights were not too cold, so travel conditions were as good as possible.

'We should reach the mountain tomorrow! What's on your mind, Amos?' asked Beorf as he prepared their campfire that night.

'I'm just thinking how exhausted I am after today's skiing,' answered Amos as he finished putting up the tent.

'No...you're not telling me the truth...I can tell

there's something wrong. Are you thinking about your mother?'

'Yes, I am. I'd hoped she would be back there with Junos. I'm also worried about my magic powers. When I took on the Mask of Air, the first one, there was no problem; its magic is gentle, not violent. But the Mask of Fire seems to take hold of me! I keep seeing a little man made of molten lava who dances in front of me. He keeps pleading with me to set his people free and to be his god…I just don't understand at all! It's as though his people were imprisoned inside me….As though…well, it's hard to explain…'

'I think it's a question of balance,' mused Beorf, looking around for something to eat. 'You've been given the magic of the elements, right? So you've got two masks, air and fire…two strong forces…how can I put it? Wind makes fire burn more fiercely…that's why you lose control. Both elements combine and strengthen each other. I think you'll be alright once you have absorbed the Mask of Water.'

'Do you really think it's as simple as that?' asked Amos hoping that this brilliant theory might be the answer.

'I'm sure it is…,' replied Beorf, munching on a hunk of frozen bread.

Just then Amos caught sight of something in the trees. A ragged doll was hanging on the end of a branch.

He went over to inspect it and, once he was sure that it wasn't a trap, brought the doll back to the fire. Beorf scratched his head, puzzled. What was it doing here in the middle of the forest? Amos looked at the doll carefully and found the name Brising embroidered in red letters on the back of its neck.

'Brising?' mused Amos. 'Do you know what Brising means?'

'It must be a girl's name. It must be her doll.'

'Well yes, but I'm sure that name comes from one of the legends in Al-Qatrum....Let me think....It's about...'

'It is a true story,' said a chorus of sweet voices. 'It tells the legend of Brising.'

A dozen exquisitely beautiful women stepped slowly out from among the forest trees. They had long, thick blond hair falling halfway down their backs. They had snow-white skin and bright red lips. They seemed to hover above the ground like apparitions. They wore long flimsy dresses with delicate gold patterns and gold ribbons were tied around their heads like coronets. They each wore a magnificent necklace made of many different coloured precious stones. They all spoke at the same time:

'We live in this forest. We were once sole keepers of this place. We are the guardians of the Brisingamen Necklace. We are a peaceful race. When humans came and cut down whole forests to make their ships and houses, we said nothing. We have been here since gods were first gods and the world first began. One day one of our children got lost in the forest. She was taken in by humans and she lived as a human like them. When they found her, she could not yet speak and could only say the word Brising which is what they called her. Time passed and as the little girl grew we kept watch over her, waiting for an opportunity to take her back.'

'And that opportunity never came, I suppose?' asked Amos.

'We were just about to take her back, but we lost her. We cast a spell on her older brother to make him steal her doll, the very one you have in your hands at this moment. Brising went into the forest to look for it. It was the chance we had been waiting many years for. At last we would have her back and take her to her own world. Sadly for us, a god called Baron Samedi found her first! He had been scouring the world to find a child with great powers. His evil magic turned our poor Brising into a monster. He forced a draconite into her mouth so turning her into a dragon.'

'That's exactly what happened to Lolya!' cried Beorf. 'You saved Lolya by tearing the draconite from her throat, Amos! Remember?'

'Of course I do! Am I to understand that not every girl is susceptible to draconite? Must she have magical power? Lolya was already a magician and Brising is a magical creature by birth.'

'Yes, but it's too late to save Brising. She is lost. You must destroy this dragon. Soon the creature will be ready to lay its eggs and her children will destroy the world.'

'We will do our very best!' Amos assured them.

'If you succeed, we will tell you about the Brisingamen Necklace and the curse of the Beorites. The two things are linked. Follow us, the Brisings will lead you to the dragon.'

The two boys looked at each other in terror. They had anticipated meeting the dragon in the company of a Viking army and now felt very alone.

Amos took a deep breath and said: 'Perhaps we should wait for Harald Blueteeth's army?'

'You have no choice,' the Brisings told them. 'If you don't act now, the Viking army will be destroyed by the dragon's wrath. You must first get rid of the dragon then the goblins. It is impossible any other way.'

'If you're ready Amos, then so am I!' announced the brave Beorf proudly.

'Well then, we'd better not waste any more time!' Amos said, taking two large orange sheets from his bag.

'Of course!' exclaimed Beorf. 'Sartigan told us dragons can't see the colour orange!'

'I asked the Upsgran women to weave and dye these

before we left. They're really two big capes with hoods. If we wear these we can get near the creature more easily.'

'This reminds me of the cloak Medusa wore,' sighed Beorf sadly. 'You know, she wasn't a bad Gorgon was she?'

'I know,' said Amos, putting on the cape. 'She would be helpful now if she could turn that dragon into stone. Come on then, Beorf.'

'As long as there's bread on the table,' laughed Beorf, 'I'll follow you anywhere!'

CHAPTER SEVENTEEN

THE DRAGON

The Brisings led the boys to the entrance of a long tunnel which went into the heart of the mountain.

'Follow this tunnel,' they said in one single voice. 'Follow it to the end until you reach a staircase. The dragon lies at its foot.'

'Thank you for your help,' answered Amos.

'I hope you've got a plan...,' said Beorf, rather nervously. 'Once we're down there it will be difficult to go back.'

'Yes, I know. I've got a bit of an idea at the back of my mind!'

The two friends entered the tunnel. Now a long passageway, it had probably been hollowed out by an ancient underground river. Beorf took an oil lamp out of his bag and Amos lit it with a click of his fingers. Having the power of fire had its advantages – like lighting up absolutely anything in the blink of an eye.

The rock had been polished smooth and the floor was strewn with little round pebbles. The boys took care not to make too much noise as they walked. After a good hour of hard walking they emerged right in the middle of a roughly hewn staircase. Two goblins were coming down the stairs arguing. They were carrying a large bag full of gold coins, jewels, works of art and precious stones. Amos and Beorf quickly blew out the lamp, put on their crystal ears and hid as best they could.

'Him big treasure, me never nothing!' complained the smaller goblin.

'Him big…him big treasure…,' replied the other.

'Me tired serving him!'

'Stop! Me smelling child meat….'

'Child meat!' cried the smaller goblin.

'You shutting mouth…you stopping me smell nice child-meat smell… mmmm. You following me… nice child-meat smell!'

The goblins came closer to the two boys. Amos knew he would have to fight and began to concentrate on his magic. Beorf, with his back to the wall, turned his hands into a bear's paws. Once again Amos could see the little lava man dancing on the ground in front of him.

'Oh no, not again! Why do I keep seeing this?' he groaned to himself.

'Set us free!' cried the little man. 'Set us free and we will serve you well! Be our Master and order…'

'This is not the time!' thought Amos, trying to keep control of his emotions.

'Come on! Come on...be kind!' insisted the little fire creature. 'We are good people...good people!' Amos was tired of their constant pleading.

'Very well then, little man. I will set you free!'

The little lava man raised his arms in triumph, thanked the boy repeatedly before running after the goblins.

'You'll see master,' he exclaimed, turning to face Amos. 'We are good people!'

The little creature threw himself onto the first goblin's boots. The goblin burst into flames, howling in pain. Five more little men appeared out of the flames and attacked the second goblin, who rolled down the stairs howling. Five became ten and then there were twenty. Amos and Beorf hurtled down the stairs as fast as they could, leaving behind the lava men and the burning goblins.

'What on earth did you do back there?' asked Beorf as they ran.

'I think I've just done something really stupid! I've set something free which might do a lot of damage!'

At the bottom of the stairs the two friends found themselves directly in front of the dragon. They stopped in their tracks; its enormous size took their breath away. The monster was lying on an immense pile of treasure.

A gigantic collection of everything the Red Caps had looted during their attacks was all piled up in this cave. The ground was thickly carpeted with coins of gold, silver, copper and bronze. They could also see sparkling rings, necklaces, bracelets, works of art, antique carvings, delicate porcelain, silk rugs and fine paintings. There were hundreds of swords, shields and bits of priceless armour. Besides the precious stones of all types and sizes, the boys could see an astonishing mountain of pearls and corals. Many religious objects stolen from temples, the work of the finest goldsmiths, were scattered among the pile. The treasure consisted of all that was beautiful, noble and precious from all over the North lands. The goblins had taken everything they could lay their hands on.

The huge golden dragon's rough skin was covered with scales and it had four feet armed with eagle-like talons. The fearsome creature had a long, snaking tail, a reptilian head with two horns, bat-like wings and sharp pointed teeth. The bodies of several decomposing goblins lay scattered around the cavern. The place stank of sulphur and rotting flesh.

Ragnarök opened one eye and saw the young Amos Daragon and his Beorite friend in front of her. The dragon got up slowly and in a voice which made the earth shake for miles around, said:

'I was expecting you! I am the new ruler of the world.

Bow before my greatness, Amos Daragon. Don't you fear death you reckless young fool?'

'Why should I fear something I have never known and which will cease to concern me once it's happened?'

'Insolent child!' thundered the creature. 'All those who encounter me prostrate themselves before me. They tremble with fear and sweat pours from them.'

'I too tremble with fear,' said Amos trying to seem as fearless as he could. 'My body trembles so much, it cannot sweat.'

'Do you know what fate awaits you?'

'What about you? Do you know?' Amos answered aggressively. 'I am here to make a bargain with you!'

'Do you think you're in any position to bargain with me?' snarled the beast viciously. 'You can do nothing to thwart me. Your powers are too limited!'

'Very well then, my friend and I will leave! If you want to see me again you have only to call me. You already seem to know my name!   It's a shame to let me leave like this, though, when I had so much gold to offer you!'

Amos quickly threw his orange cloak around him. As far as the dragon could see, he had vanished. A second later Beorf had vanished too. The dragon's jaw dropped at the boys' disappearance and she stood there dumbfounded, looking all around. She searched in vain, but Amos and his friend were nowhere to be seen!

'What can we do to overcome this creature?' whispered Beorf hidden under his cloak.

'I think I know what I have to do,' murmured Amos. 'I've got to make her believe that my powers are very strong indeed. I need to be able to stand up to her to force her to accept a gift…I want her to trust and respect me!'

'Where are you?' roared the dragon. 'Where are you hiding?'

'Did you call me?' asked Amos nonchalantly, whipping off his cloak.

'How can you come and go from my lair like that against my will?' gasped the dragon anxiously.

'Let's just say that some things are simply beyond your powers of understanding!' retorted Amos, hoping his plan was working.

'Do you dare to flout my wishes?' she fumed.

'Now calm down, don't get upset!' said Amos confidently. 'I can bring whatever I want into your cave. Let's say, for example that I wanted…a bear to appear. Well, I'd just do it!'

Beorf had the presence of mind to turn himself into a bear and remove his cloak at the precise moment Amos wanted him to appear. The dragon drew back quickly. Then she remembered Baron Samedi's warning: that she should fear this boy. In spite of her size and strength, she had not the least suspicion of the trickery going on right under her nose. The dragon totally believed all she had seen and fear was beginning to undermine her confidence.

'Disappear, bear!' cried Amos.

Beorf vanished at once.

'Do you understand what this means, dragon?'

'I'm beginning to…,' said the dragon slowly, moving back a little more. 'It means that, should the fancy take me, I can make you disappear too,' replied Amos stepping towards his opponent. 'If I wanted to, I could send you into oblivion! Fortunately for you, I am not vindictive and I'm very fond of the Ancients. So I shall spare your life and make you a gift. Before I disappeared a moment ago, I told you that I had plenty of gold to give you. Well, it's true!'

'You can make gold appear here?'

'But of course!' said Amos. 'Do you doubt it?'

'No…No…I don't doubt anything…,' stammered the dragon quite overwhelmed by what she had seen.

Amos took a gold coin out of his pocket. It had belonged to the Duke De VerBouc. The duke, who had been cursed by the devil for his ancestor's greed, had given them a letter which clearly stated: 'Have no fear. This coin is not cursed. It will guide you to me one day if you should wish to see me again.'

Amos decided to take a gamble. He tossed the coin into the air and said aloud:

'Guide me to the treasure of the De VerBoucs!'

The coin landed and rolled towards the cave wall. As it hit the wall, a wide door appeared in the rock face and immediately opened. One half of the cavern disappeared to reveal a magnificent landscape. The dragon, transfixed by this miracle, watched as a castle appeared on the other side of the rock face. It was a small stone castle with a dilapidated tower rising above it. The castle, which was surrounded by a wide moat into which Beorf had once fallen, could only be entered by means of a narrow, rickety looking bridge.

'Your magic is very powerful, young man…,' said the astonished creature. 'I was forewarned but I did not believe it!'

'You've seen nothing yet!' Amos assured the dragon mockingly, well-pleased with the effect the coin had produced. 'In that moat, just below the wooden bridge, lies a fabulous treasure. It is yours! Take every last coin.'

Beorf, a boy once again beneath his cloak, smiled happily. Amos had just condemned the dragon to death while at the same time freeing the Duke De VerBouc from his ancestral curse and his obligation to guard the treasure. Augure De VerBouc had told them that whoever stole a single coin of the treasure would be consumed by a plague: black sores and huge pustules would soon cover the thief's body, delirium and vomiting would follow and lead to the most horrible death! The duke had also told them: 'If someone should steal the entire treasure, then there would be no more need to guard it and I should regain my freedom.'

'I accept this gift with great pleasure,' said the dragon respectfully. 'I shall give you a gift in return. Take good care of it. It is the first of a new generation of the Ancients.'

Using her tail, the dragon rolled her egg towards him. Amos had not expected this and tried to hide his surprise. His first thought was to destroy the egg as soon as possible but he changed his mind and picked it up. His task as a mask wearer was not to wipe out evil in favour of good. His task was to re-establish a balance. In his hands lay a unique opportunity to bring an extinct creature back to the Earth. Inside this egg, a new creature was growing which was neither good nor evil. The little dragon, still sleeping in its shell, would be born and could perhaps be a friend to humankind.

'I thank you,' said Amos. 'I shall take great care of it.'

'Will you stop me from becoming ruler of this Earth?' asked the dragon looking the boy in the eye.

'As long as you live you will be ruler of one thing only.'

'What is that?'

'You will be ruler of your own fate and no more,' replied Amos. 'Your greed will be your downfall!'

Beorf meanwhile, still disguised in his cloak, was

taking advantage of the dragon's preoccupation and was examining the treasure. He was searching for the powerful jewel Amos needed for his Water Mask. The Kelpie had said that the jewel was among the dragon's treasure and this was his only chance to get his hands on it. Beorf had no idea what it looked like. How would he recognise it among this great heap of precious stones?

'Go now!' growled the dragon. 'Your moralising is getting on my nerves!'

'I've one more thing to ask,' said Amos seeing Beorf as he rummaged desperately through the treasure.

'What do you want from me now?' sighed the dragon.

'I should like to know what you think of this mask,' said Amos, showing it to the dragon.

'It's very beautiful….Now go and let me collect my treasure! I've got other things to do!'

The moment Amos took the mask from his bag an intense glow lit up a big pearl close to Beorf. The mask was making the pearl's magic shine out. Beorf swiftly crept up to the shimmering pearl and slipped it into his pocket. Amos quickly donned his orange cloak and vanished from the dragon's sight. Once she was sure the boy had gone, the dragon murmured:

'You will see, my arrogant boy, just who will rule the Earth when my children spread throughout the world!'

Saying that, the Ancient went through the wide door and began to transfer the treasure from De VerBouc's moat to her cavern. The boys, still wrapped in their cloaks, picked up their things and quickly climbed the stairs. Beorf carried the egg in his arms. Before going along the underground passage, Amos stopped his friend abruptly and said:

'I set the fire people free a little while ago…or let's say I let loose a force which could quickly spread and burn everything! I must stop it.'

'What, now?' cried Beorf, anxious to get out of the dragon's lair as fast as possible.

'We'll soon see if your theory about my powers is correct,' replied Amos. 'You thought that the Mask of Air was making the Mask of Fire's power even stronger. Pass me the pearl to place in the Mask of Water so I can calm things down!'

Beorf handed it to Amos who pushed the pearl into one of the holes in the mask then slowly, and with great ceremony, placed it over his face. It moulded itself to his face immediately, stopping him breathing. For about twenty seconds nothing happened. Panicked by the lack of air, Amos tried to pull it off again so that he could breathe. It was impossible! The mask was sealed to his face. Beorf hurled himself at his friend to help but even together they could not release it. Amos was beginning to suffocate. He tugged and pulled at it in vain and tried to slide his fingers under the rim of the mask. Amos was suffocating in front of him but Beorf could do nothing to help.

Exhausted, the mask wearer slumped to the ground. He was sure he was going to die. His body felt heavy and his mind kept drifting away. In desperation, he tried one more time to breathe properly. The mask suddenly changed to liquid which poured into his body through his mouth and nostrils. The absorption was now complete and Amos was finally able to take a huge gulp of air. In anguish, Beorf collapsed onto the ground beside him and declared:

'I really hate magic!'

Dozens of little snakes made of water began to form and trickled down the underground passage. They surrounded Amos and one stepped forward saying:

'The water magic belongs to you now…shall we bring the fire into balance once more?'

'Yes, that is what I ask of you,' replied Amos, at once both surprised and delighted.

'We shall eat up the fire and disappear as steam. Your wish is our command!' said the snake as he led the others to the stairs.

'What was that, then?' cried Beorf. 'Snakes made of water….Did you do that?'

'I don't know, Beorf. Some of this is beyond me. I find it hard to understand the magic myself. But, we can leave now, the snakes have promised to put my mistake right.'

'I don't know what happens to you sometimes,

but one thing is for sure, life with you is never boring, Amos!'

The two friends laughed and carried on walking towards the entrance.

CHAPTER EIGHTEEN

THE BATTLE OF RAMUSBERGET

The Viking army had gathered at the foot of the great mountain. All the Beorites were there as well as Junos, the knight and Lord of Berrion. Many men had been lost freeing these lands and King Harald Blueteeth's army was now barely four hundred strong. In front of them stood the goblins' last remaining stronghold. Behind makeshift walls made of stones piled one on top of the other, the Red Caps patiently awaited the attack. There must have been around three thousand of them. The goblins' crossbows would make short work of the Vikings when the attack began. Banry turned to Helmic and said:

'You know what we have to do now, don't you my friend?'

'We have no choice,' replied The Insatiable, smiling. 'It may well be the Beorites' last battle but it will be…epic!'

'Gather the others together and ask Junos to join us,' ordered Banry, decisively.

Piotr, Aldred and Rutha Bagason arrived first. Then followed the brothers Goy and Kasso Azulson and then, finally, Chemil and Hulot. Even Geser the Stone Marten had travelled with them to take part in the battle. Junos stood a little way off and listened.

'My friends,' declared Banry. 'We are all brothers, and each one of us is a free man. Our chiefs have never forced any one of us, be it at home or away, to do anything that we did not believe in. The lives of these brave Vikings will be at risk once our race's fierce warrior blood begins to flow through our veins. Are we to take this chance?'

'No matter whether death or victory awaits us at the battle's end,' said Helmic 'Let's make good use of our warrior rage! I'm in for better or worse, but mainly because I shall enjoy it!'

'I'd rather we sorted out this problem ourselves. Let's keep the humans out of it,' said Piotr the Giant. 'I'm a Beorite…and that means that when I start a war I like to finish it!'

'Goy and I agree,' said Kasso in turn. 'I've never experienced this warrior rage but I'll give it a try!'

'I just hope I don't hurt any of you,' cried Aldred the Axe. 'I lose all control when the battle rage takes me over.'

171

'I'll keep control of you,' laughed Rutha Bagason. 'You are my only family. I have no parents or children. If you die, I want to go with you!'

'It will be a great honour to fight alongside you,' said Chemil. 'I'm more used to working with wood than swords, but any goblins I kill will mean one less for the rest of you.'

'Warrior rage, eh?' cried Geser the Stone Marten. 'Well why not?'

'I only hope I survive to tell this story,' put in Hulot Big Mouth. 'Come on, let's get it over with!'

'Is everyone agreed?' asked Banry.

'Yes!' was the resounding cry from all the Beorites.

Banry signalled to Junos to come over:

'I must tell you what we are going to do, Junos. We Beorites have many powers, one of which is that we can multiply our strength a hundredfold in battle. We call this state warrior rage or madness. We lose our minds completely and become vicious monsters capable of cutting the throats of women and children! When the rage takes over, it's very difficult to return to normality again. We only stop when we drop from exhaustion. I've seen Helmic striking at trees for five hours after all his enemies were lying dead around him. It was impossible to stop him. If I'd been foolish enough to try he would have killed me with one blow of his paw. We become very dangerous to friend and foe alike.'

'So what do you want me to do?' asked Junos.

'I want you to keep the Vikings safely under your command for as long as the fighting goes on in the goblin camp. Don't come with us and don't try to help us! We must only be fighting goblins and not Vikings, if you understand me?'

'Yes, but there must be at least three thousand goblins and only ten Beorites. How long do you think you can hold out against them?'

'Three thousand goblins…that's just a snack for angry Beorites,' cried Helmic, slapping his paunch.

'But…they have hundreds of crossbows! You'll be shot through before you even reach them…'

'We know what we are doing, Junos. Now, I want you to go away and tell your men to keep hidden. You see, when we're enraged we can't tell the difference between our friends and our enemies!'

'There must be some other way! I can't let you sacrifice yourselves like this!'

'There may indeed be another way but this is the one we've chosen!' replied Banry with finality.

'Very well,' said Junos. 'I respect your decision…good luck!'

While Junos commanded his men to move back, the Beorites began to chant a war song. Their deep, sombre voices were raised in a powerful chorus:

We are here to overcome
We're off to fight
Free in body
Free in mind
Free in soul
We shall never bend
We shall never weaken
If the sun should rise tomorrow
It will be with us or without us!

Suddenly, the bear-men let out a terrible, resounding war cry, which reverberated across the land. The goblins stopped in their tracks and looked at one another in astonishment. After the Beorites' war cry, a heavy silence enveloped the foot of the mountain. For several seconds, which felt more like hours, the goblins remained frozen with fear.

Then the alarm was sounded, but it was too late; the Beorites were already in the camp and had begun the attack.

The Beorites invading the goblins' compound were no longer men, but raging bears. Huge as they were, they moved incredibly swiftly either on two feet or on all fours. They jumped six metres with ease and soon made short work of the goblins' lookout towers. With each swipe of a paw they killed another goblin. Their great claws tore through metal as if it were paper. The

Beorites' eyes were shot with blood and thick strings of saliva ran from their jaws.

The warrior rage, of which Banry had spoken, had maddened the Beorites and filled them with fury. They hurled themselves on the Red Caps, uttering strange wild cries. Biting, tearing and attacking anything that moved, the Beorites were merciless. They moved so quickly that the bolts from the goblins' crossbows never reached them. Their razor sharp reflexes enabled them to dodge nearly every blow their enemies struck. In this enraged state the warriors of Upsgran seemed invincible.

The Vikings listened to the distant cries of pain from the battlefield for about thirty minutes. This deadly concerto echoed all round the mountain making the blood of Harald Blueteeth's men turn cold. Then another wild cry came from the mountain. Junos turned and saw Ragnarök the dragon. In just two wing-beats the creature was flying above the goblins' camp. The Ancient was joining the battle.

'Maybe they could handle three thousand goblins but the Beorites must be helpless against a dragon!' Junos murmured fearfully.

The dragon spat her fire over the camp burning several of her own goblins. Jumping from a lookout tower, teeth and claws at the ready, one of the Beorites landed on the dragon's back. To everyone's surprise the fire-beast spewed out a stinking black substance. Something was wrong with the creature! She managed to grab the Beorite from her back and flung him against the rocky slope of the mountain. Breathing fire once more, the dragon torched half the camp before losing her balance and falling backwards. The Red Caps fled like rats from a sinking ship. As she staggered to her feet, the fire-beast seized another Beorite between her teeth and flew off, wings flapping frantically, before dropping him brutally on the ground. The curse of De VerBoucs' treasure was taking effect. Ragnarök could feel great black sores erupting from her body. Some of her scales were falling off and her belly was now visible.

Open-mouthed, the Vikings were watching the dragon's show of strength, when a Beorite ran from the encampment. The man-bear was armed with a long sword as he chased after the dragon. The dragon rose upwards then dived at the brave warrior. Just as the Ancient was about to spit fire once more, the Beorite threw his sword with all his strength straight into the dragon's belly. The monster hovered for a moment before crashing into the mountain. The impact caused a landslide of rocks to rain down on the creature. Hulot Hulson, known as Big Mouth, had killed the dragon Ragnarök with his own sword, just as his hero Sigurd had done. The great battle of Ramusberget was over.

At that exact moment, Amos and Beorf arrived to join Harald Blueteeth's troops. They had fled from the dragon's lair using the tunnel the Brisings had shown them and had set off for the battlefield at full pelt. Amos was surprised to see the Vikings in such good shape and said to Junos;

'Have you not been fighting, then?'

'No, the Beorites have finished this war for us!' said the Lord of Berrion.

'They attacked the goblins on their own?' asked Beorf anxiously.

'One of them has just killed the dragon with a blow from his sword right in front of our eyes!' replied Junos, with great admiration. 'It was…magnificent! Just look around you. The whole army is thunderstruck…the Vikings will never see the like again in their whole lives!'

'Where are the Beorites now?' asked Amos.

'Yes, where are they?' repeated Beorf. 'What's happened to them?'

'I don't know,' answered Junos in confusion. 'Banry warned us not to come near them until we were sure that they were all either dead or had turned back into men again. They called it warrior rage. I wouldn't like to face them when they're in that state!'

'What shall we do then?' cried Beorf.

'We'll wait,' was all Junos could say. 'We shall wait…there's nothing else we can do.'

In the distance, the Vikings saw Hulot Hulson get to his feet. He was a man once more. Shouts of joy and applause rang out from all sides. The Beorite had just performed a feat worthy of the greatest heroes of the old legends. No one knew that, in fact, it was really the curse of the treasure that had beaten the dragon. The sword had simply wounded a creature that was already dying.

One by one the Beorites came out of the goblins' camp. They appeared through the flames and smoke looking like demigods who had narrowly escaped from a difficult journey through Hell. They were in a terrible state, limping and splattered with goblins' blood. Some had deep wounds. Helmic had a gash in his head and Banry's arm looked terribly mangled. Goy Azulson was the Beorite who had been dropped by the dragon. He was being carried by his brother Kasso, both legs broken. Aldred had been bitten and was bleeding heavily from his shoulder and thigh. Rutha Bagason, still stunned by her violent collision with the rock face, had a bleeding nose and was covered in bruises. They were all in a pitiful condition, but they were all alive! No one was missing from the roll call. In spite of their pain, the Beorites roared out their battle song, buoyed up by their victory:

We are here to overcome
We're off to fight
Free in body
Free in mind
Free in soul
We shall never bend
We shall never weaken
If the sun should rise tomorrow
We shall be there to see it!

The Vikings rushed up to congratulate them. Tents were quickly improvised for the wounded. Banry summoned Amos and Beorf to his side and said:

'They tell me Hulot Hulson killed the dragon with a single sword stroke.'

'Yes,' agreed Amos. 'That's what I heard too!'

'And the dragon? Did it still possess all its powers? Or perhaps...'

'It's a long story but let's just say that Beorf and I helped Hulot a little by putting a curse on the creature!'

'I thought as much!' laughed Banry. 'No doubt we shall be hearing about this exploit for a long time to come!'

'Anyhow, you've just reminded me,' said Amos. 'We really should go back and fill in the hole leading to the dragon's cave. The treasure is still in there and nobody must touch it. Anyone who was unfortunate enough to take a single piece would die an appalling death.'

'That's a pity!' exclaimed Banry. 'We could have taken a few jewels to give to the folk in Upsgran.'

'We've got enough here to make some magnificent gifts!'

Beorf smiled proudly as he tipped out his bag and necklaces, rings, jewels and precious stones poured out. He explained:

'While I was searching for the Stone of Power for Amos, I thought that it would be a shame not to help myself to some of the treasure. None of it is cursed because I took it before you opened the door to the De VerBoucs castle.'

'You are just like your father, Beorf!' said Banry, laughing. 'You are full of surprises, my boy!'

'That's not all! Look at this!' Beorf showed his uncle the dragon's egg.

'Oh, good god!' cried the Beorite. 'What are you going to do with that? It's a...is it really a dragon's egg?'

'Yes it is,' said Amos. 'I want to take it back to Upsgran and ask Sartigan's advice.'

'Well don't say a word to anyone else,' advised Banry. 'If they knew you were carrying a dragon with you, you might have big problems.'

'Very well,' replied Amos. 'We'll be very careful. No one will hear anything about it.'

The two boys left with the egg well hidden in a bag. As they went, Amos turned to Beorf:

'Here's a present for you…I want you to have my dog-tooth necklace. You are far more likely to be fighting face to face than I am.'

'That's true!' cried Beorf, touched and happy at the same time.

'It will be more use to you than me,' continued Amos handing him the necklace. 'Here, take it! You now have a small battalion of one hundred Howling Hounds at your disposal.'

'Thank you so much, Amos. It's very kind of you…'

'In any case, I shall benefit as much as you since we're always together.'

Night was drawing in on Ramusberget mountain. Round the campfire the tale of Hulot Hulson, the man who had killed the dragon with a single sword blow, was already being told. Over the years the story's many retellings would improve and embellish it further to delight the imagination of the North people for centuries to come.

CHAPTER NINETEEN

THE BRISINGS' REVELATIONS

After a well-earned rest at the battlefield, the Beorites were ready to begin the journey home. Litters were fashioned for those unable to walk, and slowly the army set off towards Harald Blueteeth's kingdom. A messenger had already been sent to announce the victory and to tell of the Beorites' great deeds. As promised, the Brisings came to see Amos and Beorf to reveal their great secret: the secret of Freyja's jewels, also known as the Necklace of Brisingamen.

They told, in one voice, of how the jewels, created underground by four dwarf jewellers, sparkled like a constellation of stars and shone like the blinding light of a thousand fires around Freyja's neck. The jewels were compared to the apples of light on the Tree of Life in Braha, City of the Dead.

Amos vaguely thought he had heard these words

before but couldn't remember exactly where. Somehow, he understood what the Brisings were describing. Braha, the Tree of Life and the apples of light, all sounded familiar to him. But why and how, he had no idea. Amos put it out of his mind and listened carefully to what they said.

Freyja's necklace had special powers. Each time she wept – and she wept frequently, especially when she was searching for her husband – her tears turned into treasure. Each teardrop that fell from her eyes turned into gold or precious stones. However the legends did not relate how Freyja had tricked the dwarves in order to get the necklace. Odin, the chief god of the Vikings, had banished her from his kingdom, accusing her of tarnishing the gods' good name. A great war had then raged between the gods and many men had lost their lives to no avail. The conflict between Freyja and Odin was still just as fierce as it ever was, and Freyja had placed a curse on the Beorites.

'But why the Beorites in particular?' asked Amos in surprise.

'Because Odin created the Beorites,' the Brisings replied.

Odin had created the race of man-bears because he wanted to combine the brain of a man with the strength of a bear. He had never loved any of his creations as much as he loved the Beorites. He identified with them and never tired of watching their progress. But Freyja, goddess of fertility, placed a curse on every newborn they produced.

'But how did I escape the curse?' asked Beorf.

'That is indeed a mystery. Perhaps your father found some sort of antidote. You are the last of the Beorites because all the other newborns died in infancy. If you live into old age you will be the only remaining representative of your race.'

'But…,' interrupted Amos, 'Is there anything we can do? Is there any way to help them?'

'As Beorf's father is dead, he cannot pass on whatever he discovered, the only hope is Freyja herself. Only she can lift the curse that she laid on the Beorites,' answered the Brisings. 'Odin himself does not have the power to lift it.'

'How can I persuade Freyja to let us live?' asked Beorf. 'I am prepared to do anything to save my people and give my race a future'

'We Brisings are the guardians of Freyja's necklace. We know that there is an island, far away in the North Sea, which belongs to Freyja. You must go there to speak to the goddess in person and persuade her to lift the curse that weighs heavily on your people.'

'Would she listen to us?' asked Beorf anxiously. 'After all we are Odin's creatures. Will she not be angry if we set foot on her island!'

'You have done us a great service by killing the

dragon. Our sister can rest in peace now. Brising's soul has been set free from the fire-beast and we are happy and relieved. When Freyja comes to reclaim her necklace we shall speak in your favour. We are her creatures and the goddess has great respect for us.'

'Now we know what we have to do to help the Beorites!' said Amos. 'I assume you want to continue your father's work, Beorf, and go to this island to plead your cause with Freyja?'

'It's my dearest wish!' replied Beorf earnestly. 'Will you come with me, Amos?'

'Of course I will, my friend. Especially since you now own the necklace of the Howling Hounds...if I want to feel safe I shall have to follow you!'

'Very well!' Beorf told the Brisings proudly. 'Tell the goddess Freyja that she will soon have visitors on her island. No doubt the warriors of Upsgran will want to come with us.'

The Brisings disappeared into the wood, and the two boys returned to the camp. As they walked side by side, Beorf said:

'Do you know, I feel I understand my father better now. I wish he could be here now to see me! I think he would be proud of me!'

'I miss my father too,' confessed Amos. 'I would love to tell him how we tricked the dragon. We did a good job and I'd love to share this victory with him...'

'But I've just thought – we still have to find your mother.'

'You have your quest and I have mine....If you want, we can try to do both together!'

'I told you before...as long as there's bread on the table, I'll go with you!' laughed Beorf. 'I like food too much to refuse an adventure!'

CHAPTER TWENTY

THE RETURN TO UPSGRAN

The Beorites were given a heroes' welcome throughout the lands of Harald Blueteeth. Ourm Red Snake and Wasaly of Greenland, the other two Viking kings, awaited them with their armies. They, too, had defeated their enemies: at sea Ourm had beaten off the Merriens, while Wasaly had hunted down the Red Caps. The kings sang joyful victory songs while oxen, pigs and sheep were slowly cooking on spits. It was a rare event in Viking history to see these three nations celebrating together and it was the first time the Beorites had ever shared their table. Shouts of joy arose on all sides as wine, beer and mead were consumed in great quantities. Games and competitions were organised to keep the guests entertained. Magicians took turns to keep up the happy atmosphere of the splendid feast.

Helmic danced on the table the whole evening long, while Aldred, now recovered from his injuries, won the axe-throwing competition. Hulot Hulson was carried shoulder-high in triumph and was made to recount his exploits a thousand times over. With each telling he added more details, but he always ended by saying:

'My friends...I've learnt one important thing in my life. It is the key to my victory over the huge, terrifying and very dangerous dragon that I killed single-handedly, all by my self without help from anyone with only one thrust of my sword! Life has taught me that you must replace fear with knowledge! I thank heaven for that great inspiration.'

In fact, carried away as he had been by his warrior rage when he performed his 'heroic deed', Hulot remembered nothing at all. It was only by hearing the other warriors' tales of what had happened that he had been able to create a story for himself. Amos and Beorf laughed heartily to hear Helmic's version of his courageous feat. They knew what had really happened, but they never contradicted the Beorite's story. Hulot had become an idol, a symbol of strength and greatness. It would not do to destroy his self-image. Sartigan had taught Amos that true heroes were modest in victory and took their greatest satisfaction not from adulation but from carrying out a task well.

Harald Blueteeth's town was full to bursting and the

celebrations lasted for a whole week. The Beorites' broken bones mended at an astonishing rate. The manimals had an amazing constitution and their metabolism was quite extraordinary. They recovered at least four times faster than ordinary men. Banry could use his arm again a few days after the battle and Goy was back on his feet just one week after breaking both his legs. Rutha and Aldred recovered equally quickly from their wounds. A few good nights' sleep, plenty of food and a daily plunge in icy water produced miracles in that warrior race. Seeing how strong and invincible they were, it seemed obvious that Odin had created them.

The Beorites left the Viking coast one fine cold day and set sail back to their village. Their drakkar was filled once more with food and equipment for the journey. Banry was not as hard on the rowers going home as he had been on the way out. The drakkar sailed along gently, rocked by the waves. Junos was with them. Ourm Redsnake had agreed to take the prisoners, who had been freed from the goblins, back to their homes, but the Lord of Berrion wanted to go with Amos and Beorf.

'What will you do now, Junos?' asked Amos. 'Berrion doesn't exist anymore....'

'I shall rebuild it! That city was symbolic for me and my knights and it will rise again as soon as I lay the first stone. All my knights could not have died! I called them the Knights of Balance in your honour and now that balance is restored, we shall be reborn!'

'Bartholomew at Great Bratel will help you. He owes you a lot after all.'

'Well, it was mainly thanks to you that he was able to succeed to the throne of Great Bratel but I don't think he will refuse to help us. He is a good man. What will you do now, Amos?'

'I'm going to try to find my mother. From what you told me, I think I shall be able to track down the people who have enslaved her. Maybe she's been sold to someone decent…at least that's what I hope.'

'Don't lose hope,' said Junos, trying to comfort his friend. 'I'm sure you'll find her. You know that you will always be welcome in Berrion and that my door is always open for you. When I have rebuilt my city, it will be so grand you will be proud to come back!'

'I don't doubt it, Junos.'

The boat made a short stop on Burgman Island so that they could rest a little. After an enormous meal, a dip in icy water and a long night's sleep, the Beorites went on their way once more. Amos was no longer seasick and had even begun to enjoy sailing. The dragon's egg was well hidden in Beorf's bag and no one else knew it was there. The boys hid their elf ears among Amos' things, too. The small amount of treasure that

Beorf had stolen from the dragon was shared equally among the crew. In the distance they could just see the village of Upsgran.

It was dusk and the village was in the midst of celebrations for the winter solstice. Once more the days would start to become longer and longer until midsummer. All the houses were decorated with holly and mistletoe. The women wore long white dresses and on their heads were ivy coronets lit up with small white candles. From a distance they seemed to shimmer like angels. The scent of cinnamon and gingerbread hung in the air. The sound of sweet music came from the inn and the crew could hear the clear, haunting sound of a traditional sailors' song.

The manimals wept hot tears as they set foot on shore. The whole village ran to welcome them all back home safe and sound. The warriors gave presents to their families and there was much merriment. From the midst of the crowd of happy people kissing, laughing, and exchanging vigorous handshakes and congratulations, came Sartigan saying;

'I…happy seeing you! Beorf is being not well?'

'We are both very well,' the boy told him. 'But can you speak our language?'

'Difficult…but learning! You…ears?' asked Sartigan.

'Oh yes. I'll put them on,' said Amos.

'It's your turn to tell me stories now!' said the old man, much relieved to be speaking his own language at last. 'You managed to defeat the dragon?'

'We certainly did…although Hulot will probably tell you a different story. However, I can assure you that ours is the true version.'

'That is a great happiness that deserves to be celebrated! I knew you would do great work. Good teachers should always have confidence in their pupils. I can sense that you have some new magic! Am I wrong?'

'No, you are quite right. I have absorbed the Mask of Water and I feel that my magic is more balanced now.'

'That is good,' cried the old man, clapping his hands. 'I have lots of exercises for you to help your new energy flow freely.'

'Before anything else you must come and see something!' said Amos grabbing Beorf's bag. 'I want to know what you think…'

The boy led Sartigan away from the crowd and sitting down on a rock he revealed the dragon's egg.

'The Ancient gave me a gift. I wanted to show it to you. What do you think?'

Sartigan froze. For the first time since Amos had met him, the old man seemed stunned. He couldn't speak. He tried to say something, but the words wouldn't come. Finally, he managed to ask:

'Is that...what I think it is? Is it...is it ...really a dragon's egg?'

'Yes! Isn't it wonderful? Perhaps we'll be able to reintroduce a creature back into our world and teach it to co-exist with humans. This little one is innocent. We can bring it up and teach it respect for life. Who knows, we may be able to form a new alliance....It may be a new beginning for our world!'

The old man rubbed his eyes, touched the egg and said pensively in his deep voice:

'And what if this happiness turns to misery?'

CHAPTER TWENTY

IN THE CAVERN OF RAGNARÖK

From the cold darkness of the dragon's cave, across the frozen and now deserted land of Ramusberget, came the sound of an eggshell breaking. The cave entrance had been well sealed. The Vikings had blocked off the tunnel leading into the mountain and the great door which led to De VerBouc's treasure had also been sealed forever.

No one saw or heard the sound the little creature made as it hatched. Amid the accursed treasure arose a cry of fury. It was a cry full of the despair of a creature that found itself naked and alone in the world with no warmth or food and no parents to guide and teach it. The cry resonated against the cavern walls for a long time before it was lost in the endless corridors carved out by the goblins.

The accursed treasure was the only witness to the birth of this creature which was born immune to its curse. The little creature would be the sole owner of all the treasure. It would survive by eating insects and by licking water from the walls of the caves. It would overcome its fear of the darkness and the strange rumbling sounds which came from the bowels of the Earth. It would grow to adulthood underground where Amos' magic had caused fire and water to wage an endless seething battle of steam. It would be nameless and ageless with no pleasant memories and no respect for life except its own. It would grow wild and independent, brutish and cold, with neither scruples nor mercy. Its heart would be cold and impenetrable like the cave. It would serve no god or creed but remain proud and independent. It would dedicate its whole life to making the world pay the price of its joyless infancy and would take its revenge on the humans who had murdered its only parent.

The little creature newly broken out of its shell and weeping in its solitude and misery was the child of Ragnarök. A new dragon had been spawned in the great mountain of the North. When faced with Amos' powerful magic, Ragnarök had acted instinctively for survival. As she gave one of her eggs away, sacrificing her child, the dragon had hidden a second egg under her belly hoping to deceive her enemy. The Ancient had distracted the boy with this gesture while protecting her dearest possession, her descendants. Sartigan knew from experience what Amos had not known – that dragons always lay two eggs at a time!

GLOSSARY OF MYTHOLOGY

THE GODS

Baron Samedi: In Haitian voodoo, Baron Samedi (also known as Baron Saturday) is a god of the dead, who leads people to the underworld when they have died. He wears a white top hat, black tuxedo, dark glasses and has cotton plugs in his nostrils.

Lady in White: She is a character from stories and legends found in many cultures. The Lady in White helps humans to fulfil their destinies.

Manannan Mac Lir: In Celtic mythology, he is the lord of all the oceans. He rides a chariot pulled by swift white horses and his hair is made of pearls and seaweed.

Ragnarök: In Norse mythology, Ragnarök is the day of doom, when the Earth's crust splits open and the gods themselves will be destroyed.

THE CREATURES OF LEGEND

Dragon: Dragons are depicted in many ways in different cultures across the world. In China, they are friendly creatures which bring luck, but in Celtic mythology they are fire-breathing monsters who bring death and destruction.

Fairy: Fairies exist in many cultures, especially those of Europe. Depending on the country, they come in various sizes. Legend relates that each fairy belongs to a flower. These creatures protect nature, and time seems to have no effect on them.

Gorgon: The gorgons are creatures of Greek mythology. In the legends, they dwell in the dry, mountainous regions of Libya. In the beginning, there were three sisters: Stheno, Euryale and Medusa. Only Medusa, the most famous of the gorgons, was mortal. She had her head cut off by Perseus.

Kelpies: In Celtic mythology, kelpies are fierce, flesh-eating water horses who gallop out of the waves.

Manimal: Manimals are known in all cultures. The most famous is the werewolf. Sometimes benign and sometimes dangerous, manimals are divided into races and species. The full moon often plays an important role in their transformation from human to animal.

Mermen: With the top half of a man and the bottom half of a fish, the origins of these sea creatures remain obscure. They feature in the stories and legends of many ancient cultures.

AMOS DARAGON

BOOK FOUR

THE CURSE OF FREYJA

BRYAN PERRO

Scribo

A division of Book House

PROLOGUE

AMOS DARAGON
THE CURSE OF FREYJA

It was the beginning of spring and the trees in the northern forests were bursting into bud. The birds had returned from their migration and snow buntings and firecrests surrounded Baba Yaga's cottage. Baba Yaga, an old woman with long grey hair, walked slowly through the woods. She leaned on a long stick and moved painfully with her back hunched. Her body was disintegrating with age and she was in terrible pain. Arthritis had deformed her hands and twisted her fingers. Her joints were swollen and thick blue veins showed through her thinning skin. Long black hairs grew from her ears and nostrils. She had brown warts on her face and over most of her body. Her legs were covered with snake-like veins. Her few remaining teeth were brown and chipped. Thick white cataracts covered most of her eyes so that she could barely see.

As she walked, the old woman muttered beneath her breath. She cursed just about everything; the gods, the singing of the birds and even the warmth of Spring. She carried a bag of grain slung across her shoulder to feed the birds. She scattered it around her with great theatrical sweeps. Dozens of birds flew from all directions to enjoy this unexpected feast. But, this glorious spring day was to be their last: the grain was poisoned.

Baba Yaga had once been a radiantly beautiful young woman, married to a handsome young man and living in a lovely little village full of flowers and children's laughter. Her dearest wish had been to have children of her own, but after many years of marriage, the gods had not smiled upon her and she was still childless. She waited patiently for many long years but never became a mother.

One day, a terrible storm hit the village and Baba Yaga's cottage was struck by lightning. This was seen as a sign of punishment from the gods and as she was also childless people began to suspect she was a witch. Fearful that this was a warning from the gods, the villagers drove her away without mercy. Friends, neighbours and even her own family chased her away with insults and blows, leaving her for dead in a forest brook. Her marriage was annulled so she also lost the man she loved forever. He, however, married another woman and they went on to have three children.

Miraculously, Baba Yaga was saved by a band of real

witches and quickly became one of them. One day, on her way to a secret gathering, she learnt by chance that her husband had remarried and was now the father of two boys and a pretty little girl! Baba Yaga's heart was filled with a fierce hatred for the new family. The gods had deprived her of the happiness and joy of being a mother surrounded by children, a husband's love and the kindness of a family. They would pay dearly! Baba Yaga planned to make the whole world pay for her misfortunes. No-one would be safe, especially not these children.

Baba Yaga became a sour tempered witch full of resentment. She was taught the ancient rituals of black magic and learned to concoct strange potions using secret herbs. After a few years, she became the most skilled of the witches and was elected to be the leader of the coven. Once sure that she had mastered the art of sorcery completely, Baba Yaga began to get rid of her sister witches. They were no longer any use to her so she disposed of them one by one using her poisons.

Now her hour of vengeance had come. Baba Yaga snatched her former husband's children and killed them in the forest. Next, she threw a poisonous mushroom into the village's water supply and watched smugly as most of her old friends died. Then she sent a plague to finish off the survivors.

Baba Yaga captured Gunther, her former husband, as he lay weak and dying and tore out his heart. She then put a spell on the heart so that it kept on beating and placed it in a jar of thick liquid. She had had her vengeance! Now Gunther's heart would beat only for her and her alone till the end of time.

Baba Yaga was so thrilled with her magic powers that she began to commit countless atrocities in the surrounding villages. She stole children and boiled them alive to make potions and elixirs. Faced with this terrible threat, people fled their homes and abandoned their villages. Soon Baba Yaga found herself alone in the vast forest. In order to satisfy her growing desire for destruction, she began to attack the animals that lived around her. Once all the mammals had fled she only had to get rid of the birds. That was why she was out poisoning them today. She cursed the Spring and hated all the new signs of life stirring in the forest.

The old woman finished her murderous task and returned to her cottage. As she came in she called 'I'm back, Gunther dear! I do hope you weren't bored?'

The witch was talking to the jar which held the heart of Gunther, her former husband. She talked to him all the time.

'I've been out feeding the vermin, dear. There won't be so many tomorrow, you'll see! Oh yes, Gunther I promise you, there'll be fewer and fewer. We'll have peace soon when all this singing finally stops. Now don't sulk, Gunther. Are you angry? Are you thinking of your second wife? Yes, it's true, she was a beautiful singer

–until I cut out her tongue and killed her. Do you remember how she screamed? Ah, it fills with joy whenever I think of it! What wonderful memories we share, Gunther... such wonderful memories!'

Baba Yaga walked towards a big wooden table that almost filled the cottage. The witch sat down heavily on a chair and looked round the room. There was a bed with filthy covers; a bubbling cauldron hanging in the soot-blackened fireplace and an untidy shelf where books, ointments, human bones, children's skulls, small desiccated animals and other knick knacks lay jumbled together. Gunther's heart, imprisoned in its jar of greenish liquid sat beside the window's dirt-encrusted panes.

'We're a bit tight on space aren't we Gunther? she exclaimed looking at his jar We'd better do a bit of cleaning... hmmm... I think the last thing I cleaned was your son's skull after I cut his head off. Oh, that naughty boy didn't want to let me! Hee hee hee! He really was a wonderful little boy! Brave too! He even spat in my face before I cut his throat! Oh yes, Gunther, he was brave just like you!'

There were three loud knocks on the cottage door. The witch jumped up with a little cry of panic. Startled, she looked towards Gunther and whispered 'Who on earth can be knocking at my door? What should I do, Gunther? What's that? Oh yes! That's a good idea!'

The old woman seized a rusty knife and hid it behind her back. As she walked towards the door she heard another three knocks.

'I'm coming!' cried the witch, trying to make her voice pleasant. 'I'm all alone and I'm old and can't move very fast…'

Baba Yaga opened the door slowly. Its hinges made a loud grating noise that frightened off all the remaining birds in the woods. Before her, some distance away, sat a grey wolf looking straight at her. The witch glanced left and right before asking the animal:

'Is it you who wants to see me, you filthy creature?'

'Yes it is I who wish to see you,' replied the wolf in a deep voice, pronouncing each word very clearly.

'A talking wolf!' cried the astonished witch. 'Gunther, you ought to see this! A talking wolf has come to see us! I hate wolves…'

As she spoke, Baba Yaga pulled out the knife and with a speed and agility remarkable for her age she threw it at the wolf. The animal caught the blade in its teeth and hurled it back at her. It struck the witch hard in the shoulder and she fell down howling with pain.

'Look what that wicked wolf has done to me, Gunther! Did you see? Oh, you vile wolf! I'll rip the skin off you…' The creature didn't move a muscle but waited for the witch to get back on her feet. Baba Yaga got up and pulled the knife from her shoulder. She was bleeding profusely.

'What do you want with me, you miserable creature?' she demanded. 'Do you enjoy hurting old ladies? Does it amuse you to terrify a defenceless women?'

'You are most entertaining,' replied the wolf with a hint of a smile. 'I have come on behalf of my master to ask for your help.'

'Never!' screamed the witch. 'I never help anybody and I'm not about to start now! Go tell your master that I'm an old woman; tell him to leave me in peace.'

'Can you really be Baba Yaga?' asked the wolf. '…the most feared witch in the whole world?'

'It's too late for compliments now!' the old woman snapped rudely. 'Clear off!''Very well then' said the wolf, 'I just thought you might still be interested in killing children… my mistake. I'll leave now.'

'Just a minute!' cried Baba Yaga. 'You have been extremely rude… First you disturb me, then you stick a knife in my shoulder and now you plan to leave without telling me why you're here! Come in, you wretch.'

'My master warned me not to come too close to you lest I be turned into soup…'

'Your master is a wise man! Who is he?'

'He is called Loki.'

'L ..L.. L…Loki' stammered the witch 'You are Loki's wolf? Loki , the god of fire and strife?'

'Ye, indeed,' agreed the wolf nodding his head slowly.

'Well, that changes everything.!' cried the witch,

shamefaced. 'Do you hear that, Gunther? Loki's wolf has come to call on us... Isn't that lovely? What a wonderful surprise!'

'My master has a job for you. He wants you to kill two children who irk him. A straightforward task don't you think?'

'Quite straightforward! A simple task!' cackled the witch arrogantly. 'Tell me, why does Loki want to be rid of the little rascals?'

'That does not concern you,' responded the wolf drily. You just kill them.'

'And what can I expect in return?' simpered the old woman.

'Nothing except his good opinion!'

'And if I refuse...?' asked the witch.

'His wrath will pursue you into the next world!'

'Well, isn't that wonderful!' said Baba Yaga angrily, through gritted teeth. 'Do you hear that, Gunther? We're going to do Loki's work for free. Aren't we the lucky ones! What a pleasure it will be to serve a god who is so generous to us! Tell me, Mr wolf. What do they call these adorable little chicks whose throats I must cut?'

'It's two boys. One is called Amos Daragon and the other is Beorf Bromanson..."